Praise for the novels of Claire Cook

Multiple Choice

"Very funny . . . plenty of giggles."   —*The Hartford Courant*

"Lighthearted. . . . Her quirky voice and sense of humor are as strong as ever."   —*The Orlando Sentinel*

"Captures the reality of today's woman who juggles many parts to make up the whole of her life. March Monroe is someone we know or would like to know. . . . Anyone who has survived a teenager will understand."   —*The Sunday Oklahoman*

Must Love Dogs

"Heroine Sarah Hurlihy . . . will appeal to many readers, single or attached."   —*USA Today*

"Reading *Must Love Dogs* is like having lunch with your best friend—fun, breezy, and full of laughs."
   —Lorna Landvik, author of *Angry Housewives Eating Bon Bons*

"Claire Cook's characters aren't rich or glamorous—they're physically imperfect, emotionally insecure, and deeply familiar. *Must Love Dogs* is a sweet, funny novel about first dates and second chances."   —Tom Perrotta, author of *Little Children*

continued . . .

"It's a safe bet that readers seeking a summer fling with an entertaining book will love *Must Love Dogs*."
—*South Florida Sun-Sentinel*

"In *Must Love Dogs,* Claire Cook provides the reader with a captivating heroine, her idiosyncratic family, and love interests ranging from the mundane to the profane. All that with great humor and the innocent insistence of puppies."
—Jeanne Ray, author of *Eat Cake*

"[A] tart slice-of-the-single-life worth reading. . . . Breezy first-person narration makes this a fast-paced, humorous diversion."
—*Publishers Weekly*

"A sweet book and a reason to be optimistic about romance."
—*The Albany Times Union*

"Cook dishes up plenty of charm." —*San Francisco Chronicle*

ALSO BY CLAIRE COOK

Must Love Dogs
Ready to Fall

multiple choice

A NOVEL

·

CLAIRE COOK

 New American Library

NEW AMERICAN LIBRARY
Published by New American Library, a division of
Penguin Group (USA) Inc., 375 Hudson Street, New York, New York 10014, U.S.A.
Penguin Group (Canada), 10 Alcorn Avenue, Toronto, Ontario, Canada M4V 3B2,
Canada (a division of Pearson Penguin Canada Inc.)
Penguin Books Ltd, 80 Strand, London WC2R 0RL, England
Penguin Ireland, 25 St Stephen's Green, Dublin 2, Ireland (a division of Penguin Books Ltd.)
Penguin Group (Australia), 250 Camberwell Road, Camberwell, Victoria 3124, Australia
(a division of Pearson Australia Group Pty Ltd.)
Penguin Books India Pvt. Ltd., 11 Community Centre, Panchsheel Park, New Delhi – 110
017, India
Penguin Books (NZ), cnr Airborne and Rosedale Roads, Albany, Auckland 1310, New
Zealand (a division of Pearson New Zealand Ltd.)
Penguin Books (South Africa) (Pty.) Ltd., 24 Sturdee Avenue, Rosebank, Johannesburg
2196, South Africa

Penguin Books Ltd, Registered Offices: 80 Strand, London WC2R 0RL, England

Published by New American Library, a division of Penguin Group (USA) Inc. Previously
published in a Viking edition.

First New American Library Printing, June 2005
10   9   8   7   6   5   4   3   2   1

NEW AMERICAN LIBRARY and logo are trademarks of Penguin Group (USA) Inc.

LIBRARY OF CONGRESS CATALOGING-IN-PUBLICATION DATA
Cook, Claire, 1955–
        Multiple choice / Claire Cook.
            p.   cm.
        Includes readers guide.
        ISBN 0-451-21488-9
        1. Community college students—Fiction. 2. Women College students—Fiction.
3. Mothers and daughters—Fiction. 4. Middle aged women—Fiction. 5. Massachu-
setts—Fiction. I. Title.
        PS3553.O55317M85 2005
        813'.54—dc22   2004059101

Set in Berkeley Book
Designed by Susan Hood

Printed in the United States of America

To Jake

acknowledgments

It's probably undignified to be having so much fun as a novelist, but oh well, I'll admit it—I'm having a blast! How lucky I am to get to hang out with book lovers, the most wonderful people in the world. Thanks to readers and writers and librarians and booksellers everywhere for cheering me on and spreading the word. The New England booksellers are starting to feel like family, and it was great to make so many new friends at SEBA and GLBA.

I'm so grateful to Lisa Bankoff, my agent at ICM, and Pamela Dorman, my editor at Viking, for their brilliance and honesty. Many thanks to Ellen Edwards, my coeditor at NAL, for her insight and generosity; and to Lucia Watson, my associate editor at Viking, for her attention to detail and positive energy.

The more I learn, the more I realize how many talented and creative people I have to be grateful to at the Penguin Group. I'd like to thank every single person who works there by name, but the employee directory was too long to print, so I'll confine myself to the following this time around. An alphabetical thank-you to Viking's Mike Brennan, Paul Buckley, Phil Budnick, Leigh Butler, Rakia Clark, Carolyn Coleburn, Clare Ferraro, Jason Gobble, Dick Heffernan, Judi Kloos, Dave Kliegman, Karl Krueger, Tim McCall, Amity Murray, Katya Olmsted, Roseanne Serra, Nancy Sheppard, Julie Shiroishi, and Glenn Timony. And on the NAL side, I'd like to thank Craig Burke, Leslie Gelbman, Richard Hasselberger, Serena Jones, Betty Lawson, Norman Lidofsky, Ken May, Rick Pascocello, Liz Perl, Anthony Ramondo, Leslie Schwartz, Ann Wachur, Kara Welsh, Trish Weyenberg, Philip Wilentz, Brian Wilson, and Claire Zion.

Thanks also to ICM's Josie Freedman, Tina Dubois, and Michael McCarthy. Many thanks to Dayle Dickinson and Ken Harvey, for helpful comments on multiple drafts. Thanks to the kind folks at WATD, for telling wild stories and letting me hang around. Thanks to Charlotte Phinney, for generously sharing her talents in the hair and makeup department. Many thanks to Gary David Goldberg, for loving dogs. A huge thanks to the friends and family who've shown up again and again to support me at my book events, the best gift you can ever give an emerging novelist.

Many thanks to Working Title for optioning this novel for a movie—I can't wait to see what they come up with!

And to Jake, Garet, and Kaden, thanks for everything.

multiple choice

1

During your child's senior year in high school,
it is most important for parents to try to

- a. remain positive
- b. set firm, consistent limits
- c. save money
- d. live through the experience

My daughter, Olivia, and I were going to college. Not together at the same school, thank goodness, just at the same
time. And I knew she was going, naturally, since we'd just
made our first exorbitant tuition payment to Boston University, but she didn't exactly know about me yet. There were a
few things that needed work in this arrangement. I knew that.

Any mother who has an eighteen-year-old daughter would
completely understand why I didn't mention my decision to
go back to college to Olivia. *What? I can't believe it. Are you actually copying me? Don't you think you should consider getting your
own life?* I could clearly hear her saying some or all of these

things every time I thought about bringing it up. It wasn't that I planned never to tell her. I just figured I'd wait a bit—maybe Columbus Day weekend, maybe over Thanksgiving—until we'd had a little time to miss each other.

I sat in an ugly square chair outside my academic counselor's office and tried to justify my omission. I mean, what kind of mother doesn't tell her own daughter that she's going back to school? When Olivia was eight, or even ten or twelve, I pictured years of open communication between us. We'd never really cut the cord, just upgrade to a wireless connection. Yeah, right. The thing is, until your daughter has grown into a college freshman, you can't possibly know the depths to which your whole family will sink.

I chose Olde Colony Community College because its brochure promised "an accelerated program for adults interested in completing their bachelor's degrees expeditiously and affordably without sacrificing quality." I called my old college, the one I'd dropped out of well over twenty years ago, to ask them to send my transcript. I was tremendously relieved that both the college and the transcript were still in existence. I asked two of my former clients to write letters of recommendation for me. And, finally, after stalling almost as long as Olivia had before she wrote hers for BU, I sat down to write my admissions essay.

In 100 words or less, what light—in the form of personal qualities, rich life experiences, and untapped potential—will you add to our already glowing, close-knit adult baccalaureate program?

As I review my life to this point and contemplate my future, I am convinced that I am at the perfect juncture for continuing my education. I have juggled work and pregnancy, toddlerhood and another pregnancy, soccer and skating practices scheduled at the same time in different towns, warring teenagers, homework and family crises, sickness and health, better and worse. Nothing can throw me. I am organized and motivated, and look to the completion of my bachelor's degree as just the first step in an integrated experience of personal growth and academic challenge.

If a more down-to-earth answer is what you are looking for, please allow me to add that I have considerable experience in teaching aerobics and exercise for all populations, as well as in planning what might broadly be called "parties," but in fact includes a wide array of functions from showers to memorial services. I bring these experiences, as well as my current work as a directionality coach, sometimes called a life coach or a career coach, with me to your program, all of which I would be happy to share with my cohorts. (I'm not sure what your policy is, but perhaps we could discuss bartering tuition for some or all of these?)

I realized that I'd gone well over the one hundred words, but didn't know what to cut, so I sent it in anyway. I received an acceptance letter a few weeks later, which seemed awfully quick to me. And here I was, practically before I knew it, sitting at Olde Colony watching the door to my *individualized academic counselor's* office open.

I stood up and extended my right hand. I'd planned to start off by asking why they didn't have dorm rooms for women in their forties, especially the ones who have kids at home and are still married, but one look told me she'd be way too young to get it. "Hi," I said with a smile. "I'm March Monroe."

"Right," she said. She gave my hand a rubbery little squeeze. She had baby-fine red hair and tiny square teeth that made her look about twelve years old.

It wasn't a great start, but I was sure I could bring her around. I sat down in another ugly chair across from my baby counselor's desk, and pulled out a neatly printed purple index card from my oversized black bag. "Okay, I've already registered for three classes online." I reached back into my bag and pulled out a new pair of reading glasses. "I've signed up for The English Novel Before 1800, The Dawn of Greek Civilization, and Quantum Physics and You."

I took off my glasses and folded them up. "So," I said, "what do I have to do to get the internship requirement waived so I can add a fourth class?"

"Sorry," my counselor said around the hot-pink bubblegum she was chewing, "but a three-credit internship is one of the unique features of our program, and an essential requirement of the degree we offer." She took a quick breath, then continued, "The purpose of which is to build the confidence of our returning students and, ultimately, to enhance their value in the postacademic workplace."

"But you don't understand," I said, wondering if I should ask her for a stick of gum so we could bond, and if maybe then she might even tell me her name. "I have plenty of work experience. Did you get a chance to read my essay? It's all in there. I've done consulting work. I've owned my own businesses. Couldn't I petition out of the requirement?"

"Sorry, that's not possible. But you sound like an excellent candidate for our Business Administration major. Initiating the New Business Venture is one of our most popular courses."

I rolled my shoulders back a few times. "Let me try to explain this. I don't want to finish my degree to get a better job. I want to take classes that are brainy and ethereal and totally impractical. I want to major in something that won't get me anywhere in the real world. Something exotic and multisyllabic."

"Uh, okay, I think that would be under Language Arts. Give me a minute while I check." My child counselor worked her tongue through the bright center of her wad of gum as she flipped through an instruction manual of some sort. She stopped and shook her head. "Sorry. I just started here and I haven't had one of those yet. I'll have to ask somebody and get back to you. But, anyway, you have to do the internship for all of our majors. Check the bulletin board on the way out—and just, you know, pick one."

I managed to shake my head and check the bulletin board at the same time, while I tried to decide whether this was a battle I wanted to take on. Probably not. I'd just get the damned B.A. any way I had to, and then maybe I could go someplace a little more flexible for graduate school. I scanned a glossy, full-color internship brochure from Seaside Aquarium. A couple of cute college kids in shorts stood at either end of a large tank. *Special opportunity to get deeply involved in the hands-on care of marine animals,* the description read. I was old enough to know that this probably meant feeding the fish. And their invitation to *Hatch sailfish sculpin and/or nautichthys oculofasciatus eggs and rear the fry* sounded way too much like mothering to me.

I moved quickly past possibilities at an insurance agency, a bank, a market research firm, and a construction company, looking for a little glamour. WQBM RADIO a simple, computer-made flyer said in black ink. INTERNS ALWAYS WELCOME. I knew

WQBM. It had lots of local news and sports and weather and traffic reports, so my husband, Jeff, usually kept it on in his car.

I had a sudden picture, crystal clear, of the whole family taking a drive together out to the Berkshires a month or so ago while we listened to an oldies show on WQBM. I remembered cranking up the music from the front seat, and all of us singing along with the Beach Boys. Olivia reached her arm around her younger brother, Jackson's, shoulders, and they tilted their heads together when they sang the high parts. It was probably our last day trip as a family who lived together year-round. I felt a sharp jolt of missing Olivia.

WQBM was on the outskirts of Boston, so at least it would take me almost out of the suburbs and into the city. I even knew where it was: You could see it from the Southeast Expressway, so I could probably get there without getting lost. And, not that I'd ever really stopped to consider it before but, come to think of it, I liked radio.

I copied down the phone number from the flyer onto the back of my purple index card, and walked out to my car. I put my keys in the ignition of my Dodge Caravan and checked my watch. Since I didn't seem to be late for anything, I decided to call the station from my cell phone.

"WQBM," a female voice said. "Cutting-edge news and the best in local programming."

"Hi, my name is March Monroe, and I'm wondering if you still have any openings for interns this semester. I know it's late but I just found out—"

"Three-thirty in the kitchen."

"Excuse me?" I had this horrible feeling that I'd somehow identified myself as someone who'd be willing to make sandwiches.

"There's an intern meeting at three-thirty. In the kitchen."

"You mean I can just show up? I haven't even filled out an application." On the way to the car I'd been thinking how I'd answer the inevitable question: *What skills and experiences will you bring to your WQBM internship?* I figured I could take my Olde Colony essay and add to it, distilling the last two decades of my life into a concise and witty exposition, with the thought that, if it was good enough, they might want me to develop it into an on-air slice-of-life commentary. People were always telling me I had a nice voice.

The woman on the other end of the phone laughed. "I don't think we even have any applications. Just bring whatever you need signed for your school. Are you in high school or college?"

It was a simple question, but it made me feel about a hundred years old. "College," I said. "The second time around."

"I've been thinking about doing that myself. Anything to get me out of this zoo."

Well, I thought, what the hell. Worst case scenario: If all the other interns were in high school, at least I could hang out with the receptionist.

●

I wished I'd had time to go home and change my clothes, but it was all I could manage to track down Jeff at work by phone and ask him to pick up Jackson from soccer practice. I was wearing a black skirt and a sweater I'd borrowed from Olivia's closet this morning, and was balancing the guilt about not asking her permission with the sad truth that even the clothes Olivia hadn't bothered to take to BU were much nicer than most of mine. This sweater was one I'd given her for Christmas, which was probably why she didn't like it, even though its deep rust color brought out the flecks of gold in her green eyes. Olivia's eyes were her best feature.

I found a parking space at the far end of the WQBM parking lot. I'd been feeling a bit conflicted lately about my ten-year-old Dodge Caravan. On one hand it was paid for. And there was always plenty of room for everybody and everything, the seats were removable, and it always started. On the other hand, it absolutely screamed suburban mother, which I had to admit was technically accurate. Still, I figured the walk would distance me just a little from both the minivan and the image.

After dragging a brush I found in the glove compartment through my hair, I put on some lipstick in the mirror on the back of the visor. Then I double-checked myself in the rearview mirror, which had better light, since it was getting harder and harder to tell if I'd stayed inside the lines of my lips. Of all the aggravations of aging, the one I minded most was my failing vision.

The receptionist was talking on the phone when I approached her glass cubicle. She covered the mouthpiece with one hand. She had red, talonlike fingernails and must have been at least ten years younger than I. "March Monroe," I whispered. "I'm here for the intern meeting." She nodded and pointed at a door midway down a long, narrow hallway, then removed her hand to laugh into the phone. I'd pictured her older and friendlier.

I knocked softly on a door marked KITCHEN. "Sounds like another victim," a man roared from within. "*Entrez-vous,* if ya catch my drift." Against my better judgment, I turned the knob and pushed the door open.

The first person I saw was Olivia.

2

The ability to handle sustained pressure over a
period of many years

- o a. is called motherhood
- o b. has gray hair as its by-product
- o c. can be learned
- o d. is directly proportional to the amount of
       wine consumed

"What's wrong?" she asked. Olivia was always pale, but as
she looked at me she was turning paler by the second.

"Nothing," I said. I tried to slide my lips over my teeth and
into a smile. "Everything's fine, honey." Too late, I realized the
honey had somehow slipped out.

"Then what are you doing here?"

"Dude, is that like, your mother?" the boy sitting beside her
asked.

"Shut up, Justin," she said without taking her eyes off me.
"Why are you here?"

"The intern meeting?" I asked, as if we were playing a guessing game. Maybe next I'd try *Because I took a wrong turn?* or *Because this is only a nightmare?*

A large man pounded his fist on one end of a long Formica table. "Listen, Mama Bear, you're going to have to take a seat. I'm in the middle of running a meeting." There were two empty chairs, so I sat in the one farthest from Olivia, next to a girl who appeared to be about Olivia's age and who didn't look at me. My heart was doing a little fight-or-flight battle in my chest. I wiggled my chair in a bit closer to the table, and the metal legs shrieked against the worn linoleum floor.

"George Dickerman," the man said, bringing his right hand to his forehead in a salute. He looked at me and winked. He had a jowly face and slicked-back hair, and looked like he should have a cigar clamped between his tobacco-colored teeth. "Chief cook and bottle washer in these here parts." He ran his fingers, stained to match his teeth, across his scalp, re-arranging long strands of muddy brown hair.

"Hi," I said, hoping I wouldn't have to shake that hand. "I'm March Monroe."

"Nicetameetcha, Marge. You can help me balance things in the age department around here. Although I think we had one even older than you last year. No, maybe it was the year before."

It was hard to imagine anyone making it through an entire semester here. "That's March," I said.

"Okeydokey, I'll get it eventually. Either that, or maybe you can change it to April for me, dollface." George Dickerman looked from me to Olivia, then back to me again. I noticed his chair was turned backward and he was straddling it. It was not a pretty sight. "Wooh-ee," he said. "Got any more at home that look like you two? Maybe I could hire the rest of the family."

"Dude," Justin said. "Does that mean you're gonna start paying us?"

Olivia slid her chair back and it made the same awful sound mine had. "Excuse me," she said. She grabbed her backpack and made it to the door in three long steps.

I waited until the door closed behind her, then reached down for my bag and stood up. "Excuse me," I said.

George Dickerman shook his head. "What is it about you gals that you can't go to the bathroom by yourself?"

I ran after my daughter.

●

"Olivia?" I caught up with her as she was heading down the concrete steps outside the station.

She stopped, one foot lower than the other, and turned her head to look at me. "So what, are you actually *trying* to ruin my life?" She was wearing black pants with thick-soled black boots. The combination made her legs look about a mile long. She put her hands on her hips the way she used to when she was five and really, really mad. I fought an urge to hug her.

"I would have told you I was coming," I said, "if I knew you were going to be here. I had no idea you were an intern here."

"Oh, that's right, this is all *my* fault."

"Listen, honey, just let me explain." I tried to make eye contact, but Olivia was busy stretching one of the sleeves of a pale blue sweater I'd never seen before over her fingertips. "Please?" I added. I reached out to put a hand on her forearm.

"Whatever." She started pulling at the other sleeve, disengaging my hand in the process.

11

"Okay. Well, first of all, again, I had absolutely no idea you were an intern here. I didn't even know freshmen could do internships."

"What's that supposed to mean? Just because I might not be able to get credit for it doesn't mean I shouldn't find out if I want to major in communications. Besides, Justin's my friend and he didn't want to go by himself."

"I think it's great, sweetie." Olivia glared at me. I cleared my throat. "Well, one of the things I have to do now that I'm finishing my degree is an internship."

She looked up quickly. "You went back to school?"

"Yeah, I just started. Can you believe it?" My voice was a little too cheery, I thought.

She narrowed her eyes until they were almond shaped. "Why didn't *I* know that?"

"I was going to tell you soon. Probably over Columbus Day weekend. Maybe even before."

"So you're in college and you didn't tell me? Wow, we're like such a close family." She shook her head. Both hands were still curled up under the sleeves of her sweater. "So, where are you going, if I'm allowed to ask?"

"Olde Colony."

"Oh my God, Olde Colony? I wouldn't be caught dead there."

I was just about to say, *Gee, thanks, honey,* when one of WQBM's double doors swung open and Justin swung out on it. His elbows were locked and he gripped the metal crossbar tightly as he rode. His sneakers dangled about a foot above the ground. When the door started to close again, he yelled, "Hey, Liv, the Dick Man wants you back inside now. He said to bring your mother." The door sealed itself shut with a swoosh.

Olivia glared at me. "Oh my God. I bet the whole station already knows you're my mother. I'm going to die."

"Sorry," I said. It was the only thing I could think of.

Olivia tilted her head. "Is that my sweater?" she asked.

●

"Wow, you should have brought the video camera. I bet *America's Most Amazing Coincidences* would have been all over this one," Jackson said. "We could have won some major money." He was setting the kitchen table around me, something I'd suggested after determining that I wouldn't have the energy to move into the dining room.

I groaned and took a sip of my tea, scorching my tongue. "Yeah, I guess from now on I'll have to bring the camera with me everywhere I go. Maybe I can catch her on a date or something. Then she could really hate me for the rest of my natural life."

"Cool," Jackson said.

Jeff stirred the beef stew in a big pot on top of the stove. It was a good thing I'd taken it out of the freezer this morning and put it in the refrigerator to thaw. One of the things I always suggested to my directionality clients was to cook triple amounts of everything and freeze the extra. I mean, you just never knew when you might crash your daughter's college internship and not feel like cooking.

Jeff broke off a couple pieces from a loaf of French bread, also previously frozen, and handed one to Jackson. *Like two peas in a pod,* I thought as they dipped their bread. They even held their wiry bodies the same way, weight forward, nondipping hand resting on the edge of the stove as they hunkered over the stew pot together.

I moved my overmicrowaved tea out of the way and buried my head in my hands.

"I wonder what the chances are," I heard Jeff say. "I think you'd have to take the number of potential internship possibilities for each of you in the greater Boston area, and multiply . . ."

I lifted my head up. "Do you have to, honey?" Jeff was a civil engineer, and he loved to fit the world into tidy little packages. I put my head back down and closed my eyes. I heard my husband of twenty-two years put the cover back on the stew, and a moment later I felt his hands massaging my shoulders.

"So, how did you leave it?" he asked in his best sympathetic voice.

"Oh, God," I said. "That's the worst part. I told her I'd quit, and she said, 'Don't do me any favors.' So, I said, 'Fine then, I'll stay,' and she said, 'Fine then' and walked back into the station. So I followed her into the meeting, and as soon as it was over, she left to shadow one of the reporters in the mobile van without even saying good-bye. And I ended up in the newsroom doing some filing, so I never even got to see her again. But I mean, think about it, I need an internship, and she's not even sure she can get credit for it. So if I'm the one who quits, she should at least appreciate it."

"Do you want to quit?" Jeff asked.

"I don't know. Maybe if Olivia asks me nicely."

Jackson snickered and sat down at the table. I lifted my head slightly and opened one eye, but decided to pretend not to notice the Double Stuf Oreos he'd grabbed from the cookie jar just minutes before dinner. It wasn't as if anything ever hurt his appetite anyway. "Well," he said, chocolate dust appearing at the corners of his mouth, "I think you should stick it out, and then you can ask your school to give you extra credit if you make it through the semester alive."

I missed Olivia so much. Maybe this was the universe's way of throwing us together for some bonus time. I tilted my head up to look at Jeff, who was still rubbing my shoulders. "It could get better between us there, couldn't it?" I asked.

"Do you want the odds?" Jeff asked.

●

I was loading the dishwasher when I noticed Jeff hadn't changed out of his work clothes yet. "Do you have a meeting tonight, honey?" I asked.

He scraped some scraps of stew into the disposal, rinsed the bowl, and handed it to me. "Yeah. Rocky Point Planning Board at seven-thirty."

"Anything good?" I asked, pretending to be more interested than I actually was. What I was really thinking about was whether to bite the bullet and call Olivia, or just take a hot bath and go to bed.

Jeff shrugged, then handed me another bowl. "Drainage problems in a subdivision. All the water's running onto the abutting property."

"Oh, boy," I said.

Jackson finished wiping the table, then threw the sponge across the room and into the sink, scattering crumbs and pretty much negating the cleanliness factor. "Cool," he said. "Are the neighbors rowing around in boats yet?"

The phone rang. I was closest so I answered it. "Need me to

pick up anything on the way?" asked a voice I recognized immediately as belonging to my friend Dana.

"On the way where?" I responded.

"Your turn. Your house. Seven-thirty tonight. Remember?"

"Oh shit."

"Come on, March. You played the 'I forgot' card last time. We're all going to start thinking you don't value our friendship." Dana laughed. We'd been friends since our kids were born.

I reached over and opened the refrigerator. "We have seltzer, white wine, and hummus due to expire"—I held the small tub arm's length away so I could read it—"the day after tomorrow. And the house is a complete pit."

"Wow, that's pretty impressive. I didn't know hummus could expire."

"Thanks."

"Don't worry, the rest of us will feel so superior. And I'll bring some extra stuff. But you owe me."

As soon as I hung up, I said, "Guess whose turn it is to have her friends over in half an hour?"

"So, Dad," Jackson said, "I bet that meeting is looking pretty good right now."

Jeff punched Jackson in the shoulder. "Yeah, and about that important homework you suddenly remembered, huh, sport . . ."

"Don't either of you go anywhere," I said, "until you get everything you own off the first floor and put it somewhere upstairs."

●

I looked at the clock. I looked around my house. I used to be such a good housekeeper, back in the days when I cared.

Back when I still baked from scratch and invited my in-laws over when it wasn't a major holiday. Now I noticed my house only when somebody was about to show up.

I took a deep breath. I'd have to prioritize since I didn't have much time. I grabbed two laundry baskets and filled them indiscriminately with clutter: a stack of unsorted mail from the table just inside the front door, a half-empty box of Cheez-Its, two pairs of Jackson's sneakers that somehow hadn't made it up to the second floor. I tried to imagine what he was wearing on his feet when he clomped up the stairs, since he owned only two pairs of sneakers, then reminded myself to stay focused.

I jammed the laundry baskets into the tiny laundry room, then found space in the dishwasher for some stray glasses I'd found in the family room. I didn't let the fact that the dishes in the dishwasher had just finished getting cleaned influence this decision. A second wash never hurt anybody.

As usual, there was a sprinkling of bird seed under the oversized gazebo bird cage in the family room—birds were so damned messy. "Sorry, Flighty," I said. Then I moved the cockatiel I'd never wanted in the first place into the garage. Without giving him a chance to make me feel guilty, I headed back into the house and vacuumed up the seed with my handheld TurboVac. Next I turned my attention to the litter-box that sat in the corner of the kitchen where it always sat. Disgusting thing. There was simply no civilized place for a lit-terbox, and this one could use a good scrubbing. I picked it up and the doorbell rang. Damn.

I thought quickly, perhaps too quickly. It wasn't something I would have done under any other circumstances, ever, but I opened the oven door and put the litterbox inside. I promised myself I'd make up for it by double-cleaning the oven as soon as everybody left. Or at least tomorrow.

Every time I saw this group of friends I remembered how much I missed them. We'd been getting together pretty much once a month for years and years, first as a play group with the kids, then very quickly as a way to get a break from the kids. We drank wine, told stories, laughed and laughed, and always left saying we should get together more often, though we never did.

Marianne and Lynn were the first to knock at the mudroom door, which was the door that everyone but total strangers used. I didn't have to look past them into the driveway to know they'd driven together. Even when our kids were little, they were the kind of women who'd rather drag a carseat out of one car and strap it into another than go anywhere alone. I never quite understood that, since I was the kind of woman who liked having my own car so I could leave when I wanted to.

We leaned around the dishes they were carrying to kiss one another's cheeks. Lynn was wearing jeans and a sage sweater that matched her eyes. "Great sweater on you," I said.

"Thanks. You look good, too."

I looked down to see what I was wearing. Olivia's sweater had probably looked a lot better twelve hours ago. I thanked Lynn anyway, and turned to look at Marianne. She looked perfect, as always. She wore jeans, too, and a white cotton blouse with crisply rolled cuffs. "And you, my dear, look fabulous," I said. Sometimes I thought my friends and I were far too intelligent to spend so much time telling one another how good we looked. But if we didn't, who would?

We took a few steps into the kitchen. "Wine or seltzer?" I asked as the mudroom door opened again.

"Now there's a silly question," Dana said. She walked around us and into my house like she lived there. She placed a brown paper bag on the kitchen counter, then pushed up the sleeves of a sweatshirt that had seen better days. Dana never dressed up for us. First try, she found the drawer where I kept the corkscrew, picked up the bag again, and headed for my dining room.

The rest of us followed her. Whichever house we ended up at, we almost always sat around the dining room table. It might have been partly because it felt festive, like the special occasion that it was. And also because the dining room was the most underused part of any of our homes, and therefore out of the flow of traffic of any family members who hadn't gone into hiding.

•

"Thanks," Lynn said. She took a small sip of the white wine Dana had poured for her, and went right back to what she'd been saying. "Carly called home at least once a day her freshman year. Now we never even hear from her."

"Here, try this." Marianne passed the dip and crackers, neatly arranged on the blue ceramic platter she'd brought with her. She'd probably kneaded the platter from raw clay and fired it in her own kiln, too, but I tried not to hold things like that against her.

"Mmm, this is good," I said, to make up for my unkind thoughts. "What's in it?"

Marianne counted off the ingredients on her manicured fingers. "Blue cheese, baked yam, soy yogurt, crushed roasted soybeans, minced green onion . . ."

Dana shook her head. "So, basically, we're eating menopause dip. I can't believe we've come to this." She took a big sip of her wine, then bent over the side of her chair and reached into her bag.

Lynn smiled at me across the table. "How's Olivia holding up, March?"

"Well," I said, "it's kind of a long story. As a matter of fact . . ." Out of the corner of my eye I could see that Dana was placing the last of three tampons upright in the dip. They stood tall and erect, like little cardboard soldiers marching across a thick orange battlefield. "Do you have to?" I asked. Dana was my favorite friend, but she never worried about hurting anyone's feelings. I peeked over at Marianne, who was trying not to look like Dana had hurt her feelings.

"Dana, come on. March is trying to tell a story," Lynn said.

"We've all gotten so boring," Dana said. "I hate that."

"Well," I said, "there are worse things than boring. I showed up at my internship at WQBM and guess who turned out to be one of the other interns?"

"George Clooney?" Dana asked.

"Why would George Clooney be worse than boring?" Lynn asked.

"Which one is George Clooney?" Marianne asked. "I always get him mixed up with Alec Baldwin."

I crossed my arms over my chest and cleared my throat until I had everybody's attention. "Olivia was one of the other interns," I said.

"Not your daughter, Olivia," Dana said.

"Ohmigod, what did she do when she saw you?" Lynn asked.

"Well, let's just say she wasn't very happy." I uncrossed my arms and took a sip of my wine. "I can't decide whether or not to go back."

"Oh, definitely," Dana said. "You have to go back just to drive Liv crazy."

"I think you should go back, too. It might turn out to be fun," Marianne said. We all looked at her. "Okay, maybe not fun, but interesting."

"Of course it won't be fun," Dana said. "But if you let her have the internship all to herself, she'll never learn to share. Next thing you know you'll be living on the street because she wants the house."

Marianne extended both arms and checked the length of her cuffs. She unrolled the left one slightly. "I thought Olivia was living on campus," she said.

"Never mind," Dana said. She took another sip of wine and crossed her eyes at me over the rim, then put the glass back down on the table.

We veered off to another subject, circled around it for a while, touched down on a few more. Finally, I sneaked a peek at my watch. Lynn yawned, then we all yawned. I stood up and started collecting wineglasses. Lynn and Marianne began stacking the plates and carrying everything out to the kitchen. Dana stayed seated. "So what do you really think I should do?" I asked when Lynn and Marianne were out of sight.

"You're the directionality coach. So direct yourself."

"Come on, Dana."

Dana picked up a celery stick and twirled it like a mini baton. "Don't listen to me, that's for sure. Layla hasn't spoken to me since I told her she couldn't take a car to school. Her school doesn't even allow freshmen to have cars." She pushed her chair back and stood up. "God. Being the mother sucks, doesn't it?"

I sighed and shifted the wineglasses to one hand. I put my

21

other arm around Dana, she grabbed the veggie platter, and we walked out to the kitchen together. Feral, the cat I'd never really wanted any more than the cockatiel, was meowing loudly.

"I think your cat is hungry," Lynn said. We all looked over to see Feral scratching frantically at the oven.

"That is so cute," Marianne said. She rested a manicured finger on the door handle. "Do you keep its food in there, or does it understand the concept of cooking? Cats are very intelligent animals, you know."

I went for Feral. It was a miscalculation. I should have gone for the oven door. Marianne opened it. "You keep your litter box in the oven?" she asked. "I've never heard of that."

Dana grinned. "And you have the nerve to charge people money to help them get their acts together? I will never, ever, let you live this one down."

3

The best way to live with a teenager is

- ○ a. with clearly defined expectations
- ○ b. with an open mind and positive attitude
- ○ c. in adjoining houses
- ○ d. very carefully

People often shortened it to Liv, but I always called my daughter by her full name. I love the name Olivia, its perfect combination of femininity and strength, but I also admit that choosing it was in part a reaction to the fact that retro rock names were a little too trendy that year. Two of my friends had given birth before me, and our little group already had a Carly and a Layla. If, instead of Olivia, I'd added a girl Dylan or Cat or Jimi or Stevie to the mix, I was afraid we'd all go over the edge. We might start dressing them in baby biker jackets layered over tie-dyed T-shirts and handing them toy guitars before they could crawl.

In what was probably a reaction to the first reaction, as

soon as I gave birth to a second child, Jeff and I decided to name him Jackson. After Jackson Browne, of course, whose music we'd listened to together since our earliest days. So, I guess we ended up with a rock 'n' roll baby after all.

But back to the other one. What nobody tells you is that you'll spend years and years raising a beautiful daughter whose friends and teachers, as well as the families she baby-sits for, absolutely adore her. There are certainly some bumpy moments when she hits adolescence, most of which you block the way you did your more horrific memories of child-birth. But there are also heartening glimpses of the glorious woman she will become. Sometimes, you think this glorious woman might even have arrived.

And then, suddenly, her evil twin appears. Senior year is a roller-coaster ride without the safety bar. One minute your daughter is this amazing adult waiting to happen, and the next moment she has somehow morphed into a bratty two-year-old.

"Calm down," Olivia would say whenever I mentioned the almost-due college admissions essays she hadn't even started to write yet. "It's my life."

I'd clear my throat. "You're running out of time," I'd say casually.

Olivia would roll her eyes extravagantly. "Oh, puh-lease. Like anyone I know has done theirs yet, either."

"And so, if none of your friends had brushed their teeth yet, you wouldn't, either?"

"What's that supposed to mean?"

"Why can't you think for yourself?"

"Why can't I fly? I mean, Mom, why can't I just freakin' fly? Then you'd be happy."

It was a thought. I could picture my daughter, arms flapping, circling the neighborhood for a last look, then nosing up toward the high, fluffy clouds of her future. I got so caught up in this vision that I must have smiled.

"I can't believe you're actually smirking at me." Olivia widened her eyes and shook her head back and forth slowly. She turned and exited theatrically toward the stairs and her room, head high, shoulders back. Her posture was never better than when she was angry. My daughter might hate me, but I was pretty sure she had good self-esteem.

I'd tried many times to analyze the quick descent of these conversations, but it didn't seem to help much. I'd resist the urge to stomp up to my own room, and sit down on a chair in the family room to wait for my slight, residual dizziness to lift. And sometimes, though I'd never admit it, I'd even think that being the mother wasn't all it was cracked up to be.

I wondered if every mother whose child was applying to college wanted the same two things. One, to get the whole process over with before you killed each other. Two, to be the one who got to go instead. It would be the perfect time for us. We'd done so much for everyone else for so many years. We'd appreciate it a hundred times more in our forties than they would at eighteen.

The midlife college urge was particularly strong for me because I never got to finish the first time. I dropped out after my sophomore year to help my husband, Jeff, through graduate school. It seemed like a good idea at the time. Looking back, it was one of those hormone-driven decisions that shape the rest of your life.

Jeff had been accepted to the Master of Engineering program at Case Western Reserve University, and of course he couldn't turn it down. We were practically living together at that point. Jeff had his own room in a dilapidated house he shared with six other guys. A full-sized mattress on the floor and not much else. The house smelled of dirty socks and Right Guard, but I loved it there. I loved Jeff. I couldn't imagine an entire day, let alone a couple of years, without him. Waking up alone in my narrow little dorm bed with the tan bandanna-print sheets I hadn't needed to change all semester, and dealing with a roommate who alternated, depending on the highs and lows of her own social life, between loving and hating the fact that I was never there.

My parents would have died if they had known they were paying for half of a dorm room for nothing. But where were they when I told them I was dropping out of college to follow my boyfriend halfway across the country to his graduate school? Why didn't they at least try to tell me that I should consider my options? That if I stayed and finished college, Jeff and I could talk on the phone and spend our vacations together. That years later I'd be able to take out the love letters he'd written to me during our separation and reread them slowly, one by one.

I could even have transferred out there at a later date if two years got to be too long. I probably wouldn't have listened to them, but my parents should have tried to tell me all of it anyway. "Are you sure this is what you want?" I remember my mother asking instead.

"Yeah, sure," I answered, though I wasn't sure at all. How could someone my age be sure of anything? How could I possibly know my own mind without bouncing my decisions against the force field of my parents' opposition? I was expecting an argument, and I don't think I ever quite forgave my parents for not giving me one.

So I followed Jeff, and one thing led to others. None of them turned out to be my education. I got a job at a health club right away, which was fun, and I felt very grown-up being able to buy things for our tiny apartment every week when I cashed my paycheck. Candles, cloth napkins, our first real wineglasses.

Over the years, Jeff and I talked about my education from time to time. How once the kids were grown-up, we wouldn't need my income, or my cooking and cleaning and chauffeuring skills, and it would be my turn. I'm not sure either of us actually believed the day would ever come. And it wasn't like I hung around waiting to finish school so I could have a career. As it turned out, making money was never a problem for me. I had a sixth sense for trends and an entrepreneurial streak, plus enough flexibility to work around the schedules of the rest of my family. I'd had successful stints as an aerobics teacher, a party planner, and, for the last couple of years, a directionality coach.

As a life, it wasn't half bad, and sometimes it was much better than that. It just wasn't the life I'd expected. I supposed every woman my age had moments of longing for the things she imagined she missed.

●

I decided to go back to school partly because Jeff suggested it, but also because a new directionality client was driving me crazy. I'd been a self-proclaimed directionality coach for almost three years at that point, and it had never quite lived up to my expectations. What most people don't realize about life/career/directionality coaches is that, while some of them probably have their Ph.D.'s, the rest of us are often the recycled aerobics instructors and party planners of the eighties and nineties. It had seemed like a logical progression to me. I was thinking lofty. I was going to use the myriad and multiple skills I'd developed over the years to help people CHANGE THEIR LIVES. We'd skip the small stuff and go straight to the existential questions: *Who am I? Where am I going? What am I here for?* And the big one: *What do I want next?*

As it turned out, I mostly helped very nice people organize their closets. Or I'd sit down with them at a computer to write their résumés and we'd mail out a couple dozen of them, then shop for a power suit and play-act job interviews while we waited to see if any calls came in. Sometimes my clients and I would try out a couple of yoga classes together, or I'd design a personal exercise routine for them, or come up with a plan to get their house ready for an onslaught of summer visitors. Basically, for me, being a directionality coach was just a new twist on the same old stuff.

On one particularly rough directionality day, I was sitting at the kitchen table, waiting for a headache caused by a new client to go away. I was also wishing I felt motivated enough to do something about dinner. Jeff walked in.

"Will you pour me a glass of white wine?" I asked, thinking it couldn't hurt. I didn't have to like my new client, but I knew I had to try to feel enough sympathy for her to be able to fake it. So far it didn't look good. The first thing she did was confess to backing over her son's foot with her brand-new Suburban.

"He's fine, two weeks in an air cast, that's all. I'm the one who's a wreck," she said as she signed her name on the contract in big loopy letters. She stopped midway to tuck her thick blond-streaked hair behind her ears. It rearranged itself effortlessly into a whole new look the way only a great haircut could. "The emergency room people acted like I did it on purpose or something. 'Have you ever tried driving a Suburban?' I kept asking. I mean, they're huge. Obviously, you can't see every single thing around you."

I circled the amount of my hefty fee and waited while she wrote a check. There was something unformed about her face that made her seem younger than she was. I'd learned the hard way to get the money up front, and not to give refunds. The wealthiest people were the worst. They thought nothing of canceling at the last minute or even changing their minds about the whole thing. I opened the leather case I'd picked out for Jeff to give me for Mother's Day and took out one of my business cards. *New Directions, March Monroe, Directionality Coach* it read in vibrant purple letters. On the back I wrote the weekly dates for four prepaid one-on-one sessions.

I handed her the card and double-checked her first name on the check she gave me. "Okay, Andrea, let's jump right in," I said.

"That's Ahn-DRAY-uh."

"Ahn-DRAY-uh," I repeated. I'd read recently that a whole generation of whiny and entitled women had emerged from the daycare centers that raised them to wreak havoc on an already shaky society. I hadn't wanted to believe it, but now I thought this might be an actual sighting.

"AhnDRAYuh," I said again to get my focus back. "Let's begin by rethinking your personal priorities." I smiled encouragingly.

"Okay," she said. She folded her hands and waited for me to fix her.

"Okay," I repeated. "Let's start by understanding your strengths, your passions, and your core values."

"Mm-hmm," she said. She was starting to glance around the room, so I decided to go with the short version.

"Would you say that, while you're firmly committed to your family, you sometimes wish you had more time for you?"

"Exactly. That's so true about me."

"What would you do with that time if it magically appeared?"

"Join a gym. Get a job. No, maybe I'd take a cooking class."

"Do you find that once you identify a goal, and map out a plan to achieve it, you feel strong and focused?"

"Oh, yes, definitely. I'm like that."

"Okay, Ahndrayuh, I want you to close your eyes for a moment. Slow your breathing down and relax." She bowed her head obediently. I took the opportunity to look through the open archway from where we sat on one of two black leather couches that were pretty much it for furniture in her cavernous living room. A sun-bathed island surrounded by stools was adrift in the center of the enormous kitchen. I wondered if the six-burner stainless-steel restaurant stove or the double wall ovens had ever actually been used for cooking. I half stood then squinted, trying to see fingerprints marring the glint of chrome.

I sat back down and checked my watch. "Good," I continued. "Now, I want you to keep your eyes closed, and try to picture yourself five years from now. Tell me what you look like, what you're doing, why you're happy."

With her eyes closed, Ahndrayuh lifted her head and turned it from side to side. "I can't," she finally said.

"Why not?"

"I just can't."

"That's okay. Think, Ahndrayuh. What's getting in your way?"

"I don't want to wait that long."

"Wait that long for what, Ahndrayuh?"

"For anything. Five years is too long."

"Okay, let's take away the time factor. What do you see now?"

"Okay." Ahndrayuh scrunched her eyes tighter and I waited, sneaking another look at my watch. "I've got something," she said excitedly.

"Good, good. Tell me what you see."

"Can I open my eyes now?"

"Yes," I said. At least Ahndrayuh wouldn't be one of those clients who fought me at every turn.

Ahndrayuh not only opened her eyes but blinked them a few times, too. They were large and wide-spaced, and a blue-green I didn't think could be solely the work of her parents' gene pool. "Okay, here it is," she said. "I'm at a wedding and I'm wearing this great dress and my stomach is completely flat and my mother has the kids for the whole weekend and my husband and I are dancing."

"Okay, let's go with that. How far from now are you picturing the wedding?"

"Oh, it's a real wedding. My best friend is getting married again at the end of October. So, you'll help me find the dress and everything?"

It hit me, right then and there: both the headache and the realization that I could find better ways to spend my time. Lately it seemed to me that none of my clients really cared about finding true direction in their lives. Where was the passion, the challenge, the lofty purpose? For them or for me. More and more my clients were turning out to be Ahndrayuhs. I didn't really like her, didn't particularly care whether or not she ever found a nice dress or achieved a flat stomach. And, embarrassingly, somehow swirling around in the muddle of my feelings was the fact that I really wanted her kitchen.

Jeff walked over and stood directly in front of me, which jolted me back to my own kitchen. He handed me my wine and I took a healthy sip and looked around at our plain white appliances, our pre-granite countertops. I closed my eyes long enough to clear my head, then opened them. Jeff was still standing there. He leaned over and kissed me on the forehead. "Okay," I said. "I'm back. Say what you said before."

Jeff sat down across from me and sipped his own wine. He put both elbows on the kitchen table and leaned forward, ready to make his point. "Okay. A guy in my office knows someone who got a great financial package because his two kids were going to college at the same time."

"That's nice." I took another sip of wine, wished we'd put in that hot tub we were always talking about. Or at least the Jacuzzi bathtub.

"Maybe you shouldn't wait any longer," he said.

"Wait any longer," I repeated. "Honey, Jackson has to go to high school before we can send him to college."

Jeff shook his head. "March, come on, focus. I'm talking about you. I think you should go back to school when Olivia goes. It makes perfect financial sense."

It would have been nice if Jeff's motivation had been more altruistic than financial, but I let that go. I mean, what husband actually says, *I've spent the day thinking unselfishly about your growth and fulfillment.* I thought about my current incarnation as a directionality coach. I thought about a never-ending line of Ahndrayuhs, their superficial problems stretching out into eternity.

It was such a major life decision, you'd think I would have needed to sleep on it for a night or two. Instead, it took me about three seconds to say yes. Jeff and I chatted excitedly, figuring out the details. I'd have to work my classes around Jackson's schedule, obviously, and I'd give my clients plenty of warning that I was making a directionality change of my own. We could wrap up what we had started over the next couple of sessions, or I could help them find another coach if they decided they needed continued life support.

Jeff and I figured the income I lost would be balanced by what we gained in financial aid from BU. Or we'd fall into a lower tax bracket or something when we did our taxes next year. At the very least, we had a nice, big equity line of credit that would buy me some time. Going back to college was an unexpected gift that came along just when I needed one.

Jeff tapped my wineglass with his. "To one of our family's two coeds-to-be," he said. "The one who's waited the longest, the one who deserves it the most. May it be smooth and glorious sailing. And may it all come back, just like riding a bike."

"Enough," I said, second thoughts flooding in. "You're making me nervous."

4

Returning to college in midlife requires

- ○ a. resiliency
- ○ b. guts
- ○ c. flexibility
- ○ d. a screw loose

Best laid plans and all, Jeff and I sat down together to fill out our financial profile. Even though we checked the appropriate box on Olivia's application and included my information under *other full-time college students in family,* we didn't get much of a package from BU. We were always one of those families that had both too much and too little money. Too much to catch a financial break of any kind. And too little to ever once enjoy feeling like we had too much money.

When he found out how much we were going to have to pay for Olivia, Jeff was no longer quite so enthusiastic about my going back to school, but by then my heart was set on it. So I had to bargain shop. While Olivia was strolling along

Boston's Commonwealth Avenue from her dormitory to her classes, I would be driving from Rocky Point, the suburb where I lived, to Sandy Neck, a nearly identical suburb about twenty miles north, where an old stone summer mansion and its outbuildings had been converted to the campus of Olde Colony Community College.

I was okay with this. I was sure there was nothing innately superior about a place that had the audacity to charge almost $40,000 a year. It was like the way I was fine with shopping at Filene's Basement for Jeff and me, while we paid Aéropostale prices for the kids. While it might not have been fair in the strictest sense of the word, it was simply one of those things that came with the territory of parenthood.

All but one of my directionality clients made me feel completely expendable when I told them about my decision. Ahndrayuh was going to be hard to shake. "But you promised," she said when I called her on the phone to break the news. "And broken promises have a way of catching up with you. Once I promised two of my girlfriends I'd go away with them for New Year's, and when I blew them off to go somewhere with a guy I'd just met, he turned out to be a total jerk."

I held the phone in front of my face just long enough to roll my eyes at it. Eye-rolling is something most parents of teenagers eventually pick up. "I'm sorry you see it as a broken promise, Ahndrayuh," I continued, pressing the receiver against my ear again, "instead of a choice I need to make for my own personal growth. I'd be happy to continue to see you for two more weeks."

Ahndrayuh sighed dramatically into the phone. "A month."

"We'll talk about it," I said.

"Okay, three weeks, but that's my final offer."

It was a surprise to us that Olivia had chosen a college in Boston since she'd always talked about going as far away as she could get. A couple of nights before she left, she tucked her formerly wavy, now carefully blown-straight, hair behind her ears with fingernails painted a new shade of pink. "Just because I'm staying close to home," she said, "doesn't mean you'll see me before Thanksgiving." She picked the broccoli out of her stir-fry with her fork and placed it on her father's plate.

"Can I have your room when you go?" Jackson asked. He was using chopsticks to separate the food on his plate into piles. A shrimp pile. A peapod pile. A carrot pile.

"No. What's wrong with your room?"

"Nothing. I'd keep that, too. I could just spread out." He flashed his most winning smile at her.

"Don't even think about it. None of you better step one foot into my room while I'm gone." She looked around the table, scanning our faces for a challenge. "I'll be able to tell."

"Okay, honey," Jeff said to Olivia. He turned his face to me and raised one eyebrow a fraction of an inch. "Delicious dinner, March."

Olivia picked up her plate. "Is that all you're going to eat?" Jackson asked. "There are starving children in China."

Olivia gave him her basic glare. "That is so not PC, Jackson. When did you turn into a little racist?"

"Actually, it's fairly accurate. If you factor in the population, there are more starving children in China than anywhere else."

"Dork."

"I know you are, but what am I?"

"Shut up."

"I know you should, but why should I?"

"Low life."

"I'm rubber, you're glue, whatever you say bounces off me and sticks to you."

Olivia jumped melodramatically to her feet. "Mom, Dad, make him stop!"

Jeff placed his knife and fork on his plate. "As long as you're standing there," he said, handing the plate to Olivia. I looked out the window and tried to be rubber, too. I bounced all the petty bickering back to my children, who certainly had the coping skills to handle it without me every once in a while, and thought about Tuscany. Not that I'd ever been there. Not that I was likely to go. But I bet it was beautiful there this time of year. Whatever time of year that might be in Tuscany.

"Anybody up for dessert?" Jeff asked as Olivia stomped off to the kitchen.

Eventually, we loaded up the Caravan and drove Olivia to BU. After all the shopping and packing, it was a bit anticlimactic to be going only about forty-five minutes away to Boston. I thought about suggesting we drive a lap around Rhode Island first, but didn't think it would go over very well. To say things were a bit tense was a major understatement. We'd removed the third seat to make more room, but Jackson wouldn't sit in the seat beside his sister. Instead, he'd barricaded himself behind boxes in the far back of the minivan.

"Honey," I said. "There's no seat belt back there."

"I'll take my chances."

"Jackson."

"Whatever you do, Dad," Olivia was saying behind us as Jackson worked his way into the seat beside her, "make sure you take that hat off before anybody sees it."

Jeff fingered the visor of his favorite Boston Red Sox hat.

He'd started wearing hats more often as his fine dark hair became finer and grayer, even though he claimed not to care. "Anything else I should remove that's embarrassing you?" he asked.

Olivia ignored him. "And, Mom, whatever you do, don't try to make friends with my roommate's parents, okay? Just say hello and leave it at that. And don't offer to take anybody out to lunch. Remember, you're dropping me off, that's all."

"Okay," I said. Olivia's take on my probable behavior was right on target, as usual, and hurt far more than it should have. I'd pictured us spending this ride strolling down memory lane, reliving our daughter's milestones—her first steps, her first day of kindergarten—as we added the most significant event of her life to date to our family memory banks.

I took a shot at it. "Maybe it's because we're in a van," I said with a laugh that sounded forced even to me, "but I was just thinking about the first day you rode the school bus, Olivia. I was holding Jackson and trying to get a picture of you, and he was wiggling, so all I got was the top of your head and the door of the bus . . ."

"Mom, I've heard that story at least eighty-two times. Come on, let's just do this, all right?" So I settled for half-turning in my seat and memorizing my daughter in a quick glimpse. She was so beautiful. Thick auburn hair, skin that would be flawless once her hormones settled down. Her clear green eyes with their little flecks of gold were staring straight ahead, and she was leaning slightly forward, as if she couldn't wait to get away from us.

By the time we'd stood in line for the elevators in the high-rise dorm Olivia had been assigned to, unloaded at least four times the amount of stuff I'd brought to college when I went the first time, made sure that the stereo system was set up and the combined refrigerator/microwave unit was working properly, and greeted Olivia's roommate and her parents without being excessively friendly, we were all exhausted.

Olivia escorted us back out to the Caravan. We took turns hugging her. She looked a lot less surly now, and I could even imagine that she might be fighting back tears. I knew I was. "So call us if you need money or anything," Jeff said, as he opened the driver's side door.

"Thanks. Bye." She reached for Jackson and gave him a second hug. "Love you guys," she said quickly, as if it were all one word. She turned and walked off toward her new sixteen-story concrete home, and what was left of our family climbed back into the minivan and drove away silently.

It must have been ten minutes before someone finally spoke. It was Jackson. "Well, at least you've still got me," he said.

The house seemed so empty for the next couple of weeks. We tried to fill it up with food and laughter and Jackson's friends. We sent Olivia a care package and a *Thinking of You* card. Jackson and I went shopping for his back-to-school clothes. I was glad I had my own classes to think about, too.

I was just starting to get used to Olivia's being gone, at least a little bit, when we crashed into each other at WQBM.

●

The English Novel Before 1800 professor, Dr. Nord, was a round, sixtyish man wearing a brown corduroy sportscoat with actual elbow patches. He seemed to have high expectations. I liked that. I'd have to be sure to stay way ahead on the reading assignments, highlighting important passages as I read, making notes in the margins. I was going to be such a good student this time around.

I had an assortment of fancy new binders—rose for this class, teal for The Dawn of Greek Civilization, and navy for Quantum Physics and You. I'd also bought highlighters in four colors, two packages of college-ruled paper, and an assortment of erasable pens so that I didn't have to worry about making mistakes while I was taking notes.

The professor was saying that he was giving us only two weeks to read Samuel Richardson's *Pamela*. Good thing I'd stayed up last night finishing it, on the off chance that Olivia might call. Despite myself, or maybe because it was such welcome escape from wondering what I should do about my WQBM internship, I was thoroughly transported into the world of Pamela Andrews and her attempt to save her virtue from Mr. B., the son of her employer who becomes her new boss when his mother dies. Things were so clearcut back then. It must have been reassuring always to know just the right thing to do.

My hand was cramping from trying to write down everything the professor was saying. It was hard to guess exactly what I'd need to know for the exam, even harder to be sure my brain was still capable of academic learning. I squeezed my hand into a fist and released it a few times to get my circulation going.

The professor stopped to harass a young girl for arriving late to class, so I tapped my pencil on the edge of my notebook. I scanned the basement-level classroom. Two of my three classes at Olde Colony met in the basement. The low ceilings and stone walls of the rooms had probably been just fine when they were being used to store root vegetables and wine back in the days when the buildings were all part of some rich family's country estate. Now they felt dank and dreary.

I brought my attention back to Dr. Nord, who was insisting that the girl sit in the empty front row. The front rows were always empty—that much hadn't changed since the first time I'd gone to college. Even students my age knew better than to sit there, though we managed to pretty much occupy the second row, I noticed.

The late girl slumped into the seat directly in front of me. The professor began to drone on and on again in his nasally voice. Apparently he hadn't enjoyed *Pamela* as much as I had. I wrote the word *sentimental* and underlined it three times.

The girl sitting in front of me looked about Olivia's age. She was wearing jeans that had dipped so low in the back when she sat down that I could see more than I wanted to of her zebra-striped underwear, enough so that I could tell she was wearing a thong. I hoped Olivia had the sense to hike her jeans up or tug her shirt down before she sat, or at least to bring a sweatshirt she could hang over the back of her chair.

The professor's voice went up a notch. "And now who might like to venture a guess as to the novel we'll be reading after this one? Hint: it was written to put an end to the 'epidemical frenzy' caused by *Pamela,* which the author felt needed to be checked and cured." He hovered over the desk of the girl in front of me, crossed his arms and looked down his nose at her. She slumped lower in her seat, which only made her underwear situation worse. My guess was that she hadn't memorized the syllabus the way I had.

"*Shamela,*" I whispered slowly and carefully.

"*Shamela?*" she repeated loudly.

"My, my," the professor said. "She speaks. Perhaps she even

reads." He took a step backward, then lifted his arms as if he were about to lead an orchestra. "And that," he continued, "is a perfectly optimistic note on which to end. Class dismissed."

The girl stood and bent down to pick up her backpack from the floor. I averted my gaze so that I didn't have to see any more of her underwear. When she stood up, I smiled at her. "I was surprised I still remembered how to do that," I said.

She pulled out her cell phone, which was shaped like a candy bar, and looked down at it, then up again. "What, cheat?" she said, raising one corner of her mouth in a way that, while not exactly a sneer, couldn't have been mistaken for a smile.

Her poor mother, I thought as I walked by her.

I had a break for lunch now, then The Dawn of Greek Civilization, then Quantum Physics and You. I'd packed my classes together this way on purpose. It was an organizational strategy, as if by clumping the various roles of my life into longer blocks, I could make them less overwhelming. Instead of spending five days a week as wife/mother/student/coach/intern/student/coach/mother/wife, I would keep it simple. On Tuesdays and Thursdays I'd only have to be wife/mother/studentstudentstudent/mother/wife. I hadn't quite figured out how time intensive my internship would be, assuming I stayed at WQBM, but hopefully I could whittle it down to just one afternoon a week. And I'd unloaded the rest of my directionality clients, and was well on my way to getting rid of Ahndrayuh. Before I knew it, I might even have some free time on the days I didn't have to study.

I pushed open the door to the cafeteria and stood just inside, looking around for someone to sit with while trying not to be obvious. It would have to be someone close to my age, since Zebra-Thong Girl had pretty much cured me of trying to bridge the generation gap. If I wanted a dose of teen attitude, I could get it from Olivia.

Everyone else seemed to be talking and laughing with someone, so I headed for an empty table. It was like a flashback to middle school—though we called it junior high then—when I was terrified to approach the girls I wanted to be my friends, afraid of rejection, sensing the cruelty just underneath their cool. It was probably silly to feel that way now, I knew. At least I thought people my age should be pretty much over the concept of *popular*.

I decided to follow the advice I'd give a client, and try to savor the time I was spending alone while I stayed open to new friendships. I'd had almost no solitude in the years since my kids were born, so I should make a conscious decision to see it as a bonus and not a liability.

I dropped my bag onto a molded Formica chair and reached inside for some money. I'd had the bag forever. It was almost a briefcase, sort of a totebag with some added structure, something I'd recycled from my days as a party planner. It looked stiff and dated, like I felt. I hadn't thought about the look I should be trying to achieve at Olde Colony, even though I would have told my own directionality clients not to underestimate the importance of clothes and accessories in making a smooth transition to a new life chapter.

I headed across the room to pick up a tray. It was only cafeteria food, but I didn't have to make it, so it sure looked good to me. I chose a turkey roll-up with sprouts and shredded carrots and an iced green tea. When I got back to my table, I ate my lunch and tried to look content but approachable.

5

Balancing family, work, and college means

○ a. putting one of them on the back burner
○ b. learning to juggle
○ c. lots of caffeine
○ d. lowering your standards further than you
       imagined possible

I was the last one to get the shower since I'd be the last one to leave today. We had two showers in the house, but if you turned both on at once, nobody got any water pressure. When I got downstairs, Jeff and Jackson were sitting at the kitchen table eating identical bowls of my favorite cereal, Harmony, which could only mean we'd run out of theirs. Jeff was reading the sports section and Jackson was reading the pale blue and yellow cereal box. "Is this stuff safe for guys to eat?" Jackson asked without looking up.

"What do you mean?" I reached for the box. Empty. I'd have

to remember to stop for groceries after I saw Ahndrayuh and went to WQBM. If I went to WQBM. It had been a while since I'd seen anything but the express lane in the grocery store. I opened the bread drawer and pulled out the last real piece of bread, plus one of the ends, and put them in the toaster.

Jeff didn't look up, either. "Yeah, we could use something to eat around here that won't make us grow breasts."

"Yeah," Jackson said. "If we're going to do hormones, we should at least do something with testosterone in it."

"Okay," I said. "Make me a list and I'll stop for steroids on the way home." The toast popped up and I started spreading it as lightly as I could with peanut butter.

Jackson jumped up and brought his cereal dish to the sink. He grabbed my upper arm with both hands and pulled himself in for an awkward little hug. "Way to go, Mom. You made a joke. I thought you were gonna make me read the ingredients out loud and take a short quiz on substance abuse." I stood on my tiptoes so I could kiss him on his forehead.

Jeff put his bowl in the sink. He dropped his chin so he could look over his reading glasses at Jackson's feet. "Are those my new sneakers?"

"Mom told me they were mine."

"I did?" The toast needed more peanut butter. I reached for the jar.

Jackson shook his head at his father. "I knew she wasn't listening. She had that glazed look in her eyes."

I chewed then swallowed, washing it down with a sip of coffee. "Then why did you listen to me?"

"Do you want them back, Dad?" Jackson leaned down and started working on a shoelace.

"After your smelly feet have been in them? I don't think so." Jeff gave Jackson a pat on the back. "Come on, we'll both be late."

Jackson ran up to his room to grab his backpack. "So," Jeff said, zipping up the case of his laptop, "have you decided what you're going to do about the internship?"

"Well, I was hoping to start by listening to some good advice from my husband."

Jeff shrugged his shoulders and dropped his head to one side, managing to look just like Jackson. "Hmm . . . it's a tough one. I don't know what you should do. Run? Maybe you can get into a witness protection plan, though they're not technically designed for this sort of thing."

"Come on," I said.

Jeff pushed up the sleeve of his jacket and checked his watch. I waited. He looked up and we stared at each other. "No way," he said. "I've been here. Whatever I say, you'll jump down my throat."

I grabbed the peanut butter knife a little too tightly. I yanked out the door of the dishwasher and released my grip on the knife so it dropped into the silverware compartment. Jeff put his hand on my shoulder and I turned around to face him. "Thanks a lot," I said.

"Listen. I don't want to fight. Whatever you decide, I'll back you up. Go back to WQBM, don't go. I'll even go with you, put in a few good words about you to Olivia." He smiled and I tried not to smile back. "But it's your decision."

I wasn't sure exactly what reaction I'd been hoping for, but I knew this was as good as it was going to get. I mean, what husband who is about to be late for work actually says, *Your problems are my problems. I won't be able to think of anything else until we work this out. I'd simply worry about you too much. So let's just sit right down and figure this out now.*

I decided to go for the next best thing. I gave Jeff a fairly calculated kiss on the lips and said, "Never mind. I'll figure it out. But can you stop and get groceries after you pick Jackson up from soccer?"

Jeff reached over to the counter for his laptop case and lifted the strap over his shoulder. "Don't think I don't know what that kiss was for."

"What?"

"That was your butter-me-up-to-buy-groceries kiss. I'd know it anywhere."

I leaned forward and kissed him again. "How's it working?"

Jeff reached his arms around me. "You're incorrigible."

"Is that a yes?"

"All right."

"Thanks. And maybe another pair of sneakers for yourself?"

"Don't push your luck. Besides, you'd only give them away on me."

Jackson came in wearing his backback and stopped long enough for me to give him a hug. "Mom, where's Flighty?" he asked.

"Oops," I said. "I think he might be in the garage."

●

Ahndrayuh's son, Clark, was at school and her daughter, Hillary, was at daycare, and I was teaching Ahndrayuh that it was possible to get a mental break as well as a physical work-out even when they were home. Of course, since they weren't home, we were going to have to pretend. I wondered if this might be too much of a stretch for Ahndrayuh.

"Think of it as circuit training," I said. "We'll set my watch for ten minutes and do some abdominal work while we pretend they're watching cartoons right in the same room with us." I handed her a purple exercise mat that I'd had silkscreened to match my business cards and opened up an identical one for myself.

Ahndrayuh stretched out on her back on her mat. "Okay," I said. "Show me what you usually do for your abs." Ahndrayuh began doing full sit-ups with straight legs, so I put out a hand to stop her. "Those can be a little bit rough on your back. The ones I'm going to show you are more effective, too." I would have said the last part whether it was true or not, because women Ahndrayuh's age never worried about hurting their backs. It was only when they got to be my age that they wished they'd been more careful.

I set my watch for ten minutes, and helped Ahndrayuh through a series of crunches and reverse curls for her rectus abdominus muscles, making sure she kept her knees bent and her feet flat on the floor, then added some twists to work her external obliques. As soon as she mastered the correct form for an exercise, I'd slide over to my own mat and sneak in some reps myself. I didn't get quite the workout that she did, but I wasn't paying for it, either.

The alarm on my watch went off and Ahndrayuh flopped back on her mat and clutched her stomach with both hands. "Wow, I felt that," she said. "You can't quit now—you're just starting to make progress with me." She yanked up her T-shirt and peeked underneath. "How about if you just keep me and get rid of all your other clients?"

I ignored her. It was the only way. "Okay, up, up, up. Time

for the next circuit." I jumped energetically to my feet, untied my jacket from my waist, and started to put it on.

Ahndrayuh rolled over to her side as if she were about to take a nap.

I clapped my hands together briskly. "Come on, I mean right now. Jump up, grab a jacket. Oh, and we're going to need your stroller and two of the kids' stuffed animals."

We stood in the open doorway of the garage, and while Ahndrayuh zipped up her jacket, I buckled a stegosaurus into the seat of the stroller and placed the teddy bear's paw in one of my hands. "How often do you take the kids out for a walk?" I asked.

"Well, I'd do it all the time if they behaved like that," Ahndrayuh said with a giggle, and I wondered for the first time if she might have grown on me just a little bit. Nah, it was probably just that I knew I'd be rid of her soon. "It's just too hard, so I usually wait until the weekend when my husband is home and make him do it."

"That's because you're thinking of it as work. If you change your mindset, you'll realize it's really an opportunity. I never would have survived when my kids were as young as yours are if I hadn't been able to sneak in a workout when I needed one." I rolled the stroller forward and back a couple of times. "Okay, first of all, you have the aerobic conditioning of a brisk walk, with the added bonus of all this extra weight you're pushing, which will help you burn some extra calories, plus give you a great upper-body workout." I gave the teddy bear a little swing. "And Clark's old enough to start building exercise into his life, too."

"I'm not sure I think exercise is very important for kids. It's not like they're worried about fitting into their clothes or anything."

I was curious. "What do you think is important for kids?"

"Well," she said. "I think there are three important things." She grabbed three fingers of one hand with her other hand. I kept us moving out through the garage doors. "Lots of toys . . . plenty of friends . . . birthday candles that don't blow out . . . rooms of their own . . . how many was that?"

"That was three," I said. I set the alarm on my watch again.

Ahndrayuh stretched and yawned. "Then I lied. The most important thing of all is to be a kid as long as you can, or you'll spend the rest of your life wishing you still were one."

I had a frightening urge to write that down. I shook it off and pushed the start button on the stopwatch. "Okay," I said, "let's see how many times we can go around this cul de sac in twenty minutes."

"You're kidding."

"Why?"

"My neighbors are going to think I'm totally bizarre."

"So? That's half the fun of it." I held the teddy bear out to her. "Do you want to hold Clark's hand or shall I?"

To her credit, Ahndrayuh smiled, though she didn't take the stuffed animal. I picked up the pace and she stayed with me, although I also noticed I was the one pushing the stroller. Smoothly, I stepped back and let Ahndrayuh take it. She bumped the stroller down to the street. I made sure the teddy bear looked both ways before we crossed over to the other side of the street, then got back up on the sidewalk for another lap.

"You're doing great," I said. "How's it feel?"

Ahndrayuh stopped and tucked her hair behind her ears. "Well, it's fine now," she said, "but to tell you the truth I think it would be much harder with real kids."

6

If you weren't a very good student the first
time

- a. it was because you had more parties to
  go to then
- b. it only means you hadn't yet discovered
  your inner student
- c. you can make up for it now
- d. oh, no, it could happen again

I stopped at home for a quick change after leaving Ahn-drayuh's house. I threw a couple of kitty treats to Feral and topped off the food in Flighty's dish to make up for leaving him in the garage for a couple of nights. Why was this kind of thing always my fault? Okay, technically I'd put him out there, but it wasn't like anyone else had noticed, either. And it was a very nice garage.

I couldn't put my finger on the exact moment I made the decision to go back to WQBM. It was more of a gradual realization. Perhaps my session with Ahndrayuh impaired my judgment. Or maybe I was still deluding myself, just a little, that this could somehow work. I'd picked up the phone to call Olivia several times. But each time I chickened out and put the phone back down. I'd even thought about calling WQBM today to say I wouldn't be coming back, not that I imagined anyone would particularly care or even notice, except my daughter who would be thrilled.

But I was also thinking about the hassle of having to find another internship, and quickly. In the end, it was probably a combination of wishful thinking that Olivia might somehow come around, coupled with a previously undiscovered streak of masochism, that sent me driving up the Southeast Expressway toward the radio station again.

As I walked by her, I noticed the WQBM receptionist had squared off the ends of her fingernails and changed the polish to a rhododendron pink. I headed for the kitchen and stood outside the door and listened. Olivia was laughing. She'd always had a great laugh, rich and melodic, with a touch of wantonness, as if she were just about to cross the line into hilarity and might not be able to reign herself back in. It was a laugh that always made me want to laugh, too, and I probably appreciated it all the more because Olivia so rarely let down her cool.

I gave the door a push and it swung inward with a creak. The three interns looked up from their seats at the kitchen table. Olivia stopped laughing as soon as she saw me. The other girl said, "Hey."

The boy, whose name I knew I'd heard but couldn't remember, had his chair tipped back on two legs and his arms stretched wide for balance. "Hey," he said.

"Hey," I said back.

Olivia mumbled something under her breath.

"Excuse me?" I said.

Olivia gave me her most sullen look. I noticed she was wearing a pair of silver earrings I'd never seen before. "Just don't say 'hey,' okay?" she said.

I took a deep breath in and let it out slowly. I was absolutely positive that saying, *Don't you dare take that tone with me, young lady,* wasn't where I wanted to go. A part of me wanted to say it anyway, just for the quick cheap thrill of it. I settled for ignoring her and sat down at the table.

"Dude," the boy intern said finally. "So, Mrs. Mom, what was Liv like as a baby?"

"Knock it off, Justin," Olivia said.

"Call me March," I said, sliding into the chair closest to the door. "And it's nice to meet you, Justin."

"For the record," he said in a completely unbelievable English accent, "let me just say that I couldn't be happier."

"Thanks," I said, overlooking the possibility of sarcasm. I turned to the other intern. "Hi. And what's your name?"

"Caitlin," she said. I might have been imagining it, but it looked like she could have given me a slight smile. She had a pretty face, but it was surrounded by kind of lifeless brown hair, which she'd made worse by weighing it down with gel and adding an assortment of tiny, multicolored clips.

"So, what's on the agenda for today?" I asked brightly, looking at Caitlin and Justin.

Justin brought his chair back down and started beating a tribal rhythm on the table top. He had fine blond hair that hung in a jaw-length fringe. "Dude, that doesn't sound like life at the BM. Mostly we just sit around and wait for the Dick Man to show."

The door creaked open again and the receptionist waved a piece of paper at us. "The boss just called in," she said. "Something came up." She waited while the kids rolled their eyes. "Okay, one of you is supposed to go out and clean the mobile van, somebody else is supposed to go upstairs and sort through the old records and pull anything you can find from 1963 for the oldies show, and anybody else who's here is supposed to help out on a show."

●

I guess I could have been happy that Olivia picked working with me on a show over cleaning out the mobile van, but I was too furious with her to see it that way. I waited until Justin and Caitlin were out of earshot. "Don't you ever, ever speak to me like that again," I hissed as we headed out into the hallway.

"Sorry," she said, stretching out the word so I'd know she didn't really mean it.

I stopped and crossed my arms over my chest. "Listen. Let's clear this up right now. If I'm going to ruin your life by keeping this internship, you're going to have to come out and tell me that so I can find something else before it's too far into the semester to get anything." The long sentence left me completely without air, so I gulped some in.

Olivia crossed her arms over her chest. "No way. You're not putting that guilt trip on me."

We stared at each other. A door opened and a woman poked her head out and stage-whispered, "Are you my interns?" We took a moment to read the sign on the door, which said KARYN'S KARMIC KORNER in squiggly red marker on a whiteboard. We nodded. "Hurry," she hissed. She disappeared back inside and the door clicked shut again.

Olivia turned the knob and we walked into a long narrow windowless room with three foam-covered microphones sitting in a row on a wood-grained table. The woman, a very small birdlike woman in a very large scarflike dress, sat at the table talking into a telephone. "Fine then," she said in a surprisingly deep voice. She slammed the phone down.

"Excuse me, Karyn?" I said.

"That's Kah-RYNN," she said. "Accent on the second syllable."

"Sorry," I said, "Kah-RYNN." *Didn't anyone anywhere pronounce their names normally anymore?* I wondered.

"Actually, it's Rhonda," she said in the same resonant voice. A real radio voice.

"So is Karyn like your stage name?" Olivia asked. She always made this kind of connection before I did. I was still stuck on the dress. I wanted to ask this woman if she was wearing Karyn's dress or if she'd just lost a lot of weight, maybe one hundred pounds or so, but I figured it was none of my business. The dress was sort of tie-dyed chiffon and sleeveless. The oversized armholes exposed most of a yellowed bra and made her arms look like twigs.

"You got it. *Rhonda's Karmic Korner*? I don't think so. Listen, we have a problem."

I thought she should at least know our names before Olivia and I became *we* with her. "Hi, I'm March Monroe and this is my . . . this is Olivia."

"Great. Listen, my guest just canceled. She was stuck in traffic and the vibes were all wrong. Mercury in retrograde will do that to you. So she turned around and went home."

"What are you going to do?" I asked, carefully avoiding the use of the word *we*.

Karyn scratched one thin arm, leaving flaky trails on her white skin, while she thought. "I guess I'll have to do a past-life regression," she said when she was finished. "Yeah, that'll work. Okay, and by the way, you're my faces. I'm so much better when I have faces."

"Three minutes," a disembodied voice said.

I jumped. My heart skipped a beat then made up for lost time. "What was that?" I asked.

"Mom, give me a break. It was just the producer." Olivia shook her head. "What do faces have to do?" she asked Karyn.

"Sit in front of a microphone and look interested in everything I say. It helps me to connect. And talk, but only if I need you. And just remember it's radio. Don't nod your head or make gestures. And keep your mouth close to the microphone but not on it."

"Two minutes," the voice said. We all moved quickly to the chairs in front of the microphones. My heartbeat was still slightly erratic.

"Do you have a choice of past lives to regress to, or do you have only one?" I whispered.

"Lately it's been an eighteenth-century gentleman named Henry."

"Wow," I whispered. "What a small world. I've been taking a course called The English Novel Before 1800."

"What did you say your name was?"

"March Monroe."

●

Karyn leaned into the microphone.

"Greetings and welcome to *Karyn's Karmic Korner*. I am here today with March Monroe, noted scholar and expert on the eighteenth century, who, with her research assistant, will verify the authenticity of the past-life regression you are about to witness live on WQBM Radio. But first, a word from our local sponsors."

"Excuse me," I said. "But I'm not really comfortable being portrayed . . ."

Karyn put her elbows on the table and leaned forward. I could see right down the front of her dress. She really should buy better bras if she was going to let them show like that. "Shh," she said, shaping her mouth like a little beak. "Okay, give me something from one of the books you read for school."

"Excuse me?" I said again.

"Come on. Give me a character or two and something that happens."

"Well, in *Pamela,* there's a servant who's trying to protect her virtue from her new employer."

"How?"

"Well, she sobs and faints a lot and . . ."

"Perfect."

"Wait a minute. You're going to fake a past-life regression? I mean, don't you believe in them?"

"Of course I believe in them," Karyn said. "I can *do* them. But, what, you think I can turn it on and off like a faucet?"

"Ten seconds," the same disembodied voice said. It was full and rich, like some heavenly utterance from above. It made me think of *The Wizard of Oz.* I wondered if it was a recording, if some unimposing, thin-voiced person was actually back behind a curtain somewhere pushing a button every time a ten-second warning was needed.

Karyn leaned into her microphone again. "And we're back

live with *Karyn's Karmic Korner*. And this is Karyn. I am about to attempt to reach back to a former life I lived in the eighteenth century, as a man who tried to victimize his young female servant. In this life I was known as . . ." Karyn paused, looked at my face, and mouthed, "Who?"

"Mr. B.," I mouthed.

"Mr. T.," she said. "Now, if we can have absolute silence both here in the studio as well as at home, I will begin." Olivia and I snuck a peek at each other. Olivia looked away as soon as she saw me looking. She reached back and divided her ponytail in half with her fingers, then pulled each handful of hair in the opposite direction until the ponytail sat higher on her head.

Karyn put her head down on the table, then lifted it up. She ran her index finger along the top of her lip from the center and out to one cheek, then out to the other, as if she were stroking a mustache. "I'll do you no harm, Pamela. Do not be afraid of me," she said in an English accent not much better than Justin's. "It is simply that you are the most beautiful woman I have ever seen, far too beautiful to be a mere servant."

Her accent might not have been much, but she wasn't too far off in terms of story line. "What, Pamela," she continued in her deep voice. "Have you fainted, fainted dead away? Or is that merely a ploy to protect your young virtue from my sweet kisses?"

I felt a slight pressure on the top of my shoe. I knew right away it wasn't a ghost or a spirit. It was Olivia and she was stepping on my foot to say, *Can you believe this?* It was just a small sign and I didn't want to read too much into it, but I wondered if there might be hope for my daughter and me and our internship yet.

We sat silently through the rest of the past-life regression, trying not to look at each other. A couple of ads cut in, and Karyn slumped forward on the table during them, her head buried in her arms, her bony back so exposed you could count each vertebra. Olivia rolled her eyes at me and I nodded. Some disconnected chitchat followed the regression, and we tried to be good faces.

Finally, after what might well have been the longest half hour I'd ever spent, Karyn leaned into the microphone, dropped her voice even lower, and said, "Until next week, this is *Karyn's Karmic Korner*." She paused for a moment as New Age elevator music flowed into the room from somewhere. "And just remember: Karma is a boomerang."

I wrote it down in the notebook I always carried with me as soon as I got back out into the hallway. You just never knew when you might be able to use a little nugget like that.

Olivia stopped beside me and watched. "Remember when I was little and whenever you and Dad had people over, I'd sneak down and sit on the stairs and write down everything you said? And read it back to you the next day at breakfast?"

"I never should have given you my old *Harriet the Spy* book. It was all my fault."

"Yeah, well." Olivia yawned and glanced down at her watch. She looked back up. "How's Dad? I was thinking I might call him and invite him out to lunch."

I felt a flash of jealousy but forced myself to smile. "He's fine. He misses you, though. Jackson, too."

"I talk to Jackson all the time."

"You do?"

"Yeah, we IM each other. How else would he know what to wear to school?"

I swallowed down another mouthful of jealousy. "No wonder he looks so great these days," I said.

Olivia narrowed her green eyes at me. "What's that supposed to mean?"

"Nothing. He just looks great, that's all."

"God, I can't even talk to you." She shook her head a couple of times, flipping her ponytail back and forth. "I gotta go. I have a test to cram for."

"Okay. Bye, honey," I said to my daughter as she walked away from me.

A door opened behind me, and the disembodied voice from the show said, "Pretty awful, isn't she?"

I turned. The man was about my age, and the rest of him definitely lived up to the voice. He had longish salt-and-pepper hair and a crooked smile that crinkled the corners of his blue eyes. Very blue eyes.

"You know my daughter?" I asked.

He laughed and it was that same deep, rich sound. A real radio laugh. "No, I meant Karyn. She's enough to make you stop believing in your horoscope."

The man connected to the voice even had a name—David Callahan. "How about a tour?" he asked, after we finished introducing ourselves.

"Sure," I answered wittily.

"This," he said as soon as I followed him into the production studio, "is called a three-sixty. It's a voice editing machine. You can listen to the interviews and edit out the *ums* and *uhs*."

"How does it work?"

"See, you just wind the knob counterclockwise . . . and then you take out the parts you don't want."

"That's amazing. It's just like an Etch A Sketch."

He laughed. "That's funny. I haven't thought of Etch A Sketches in years."

"It does, though, doesn't it? I think they should make portable ones. So you could get rid of all the things you didn't mean to say."

"Do you say a lot of things you don't mean to?"

"Only when I share an internship with my daughter."

David peered through the glass window of the production studio into the connected conference room Karyn had done her show in. "So that really was your daughter? I thought you two looked alike. That must be interesting, both of you being interns here at once."

"Oh, you have no idea." I leaned a little closer so that I could see what he'd seen during the show. I was suddenly aware of being too close to him. I pulled back, but not before I noticed that he smelled good. "How come I couldn't see you?" I asked.

"When I do Karyn's show, I keep the lights down in here and slide back out of the way. I have a hard time watching and maintaining my professional demeanor."

"I bet." He was still smiling at me, so I tried to think of something that would keep the conversation going. "I'm actually kind of surprised she has a show. I mean, aren't there some kind of standards?"

"Around here? Surely you jest. Anyway, it's broker time."

"What's that?"

"Broker time means you pay a couple hundred dollars a

show to be on the air. Plus you pay your own producer-engineer, a job that underpaid individuals like myself are only too happy to pick up. And then you sell your own ads, and eventually, theoretically, you might even make a profit before hell freezes over."

"Wow, I had no idea."

"Yeah, we've had a few beauties around here. A home fix-it show by a carpenter who got so desperate for guests that he invited his son on to talk about being student of the month at Marshbury Middle School."

I laughed. He was really fun to listen to.

David shook his head. "Yeah, wait till you've been around for a while. Little by little you'll start catching on to all the trade secrets. But that's all you'll get from me. You'll have to pick up the rest on your own."

"Oh, come on. Just give me one more." I could actually hear the flirty tone in my voice. I didn't even sound that out of practice.

"Okay, one. You know those helicopters the reporters call in the rush hour traffic reports from?"

"Yeah."

"Well, this is how they do it here." David Callahan leaned into a microphone and pounded his chest with alternating fists. "We're up in the WQBM helicopter and it's looking worse by the minute down there on Route 3 . . ."

I couldn't quite seem to stop laughing. "Sorry," I said, running my finger under one eye before the tears could ruin my mascara. "I know it's not *that* funny. It's been a long week, I guess."

David grabbed a worn leather jacket from a hook on the

wall. He turned and frowned at me. "What do you mean, it wasn't that funny?"

I raised my eyebrows. "Oops," I said.

He smiled. "That was some of my best material."

I smiled back. "Then I guess you'll have to step it up a little." I glanced over his shoulder at the clock on the wall. "Ohmigod, is that clock right?"

David reached over and opened the door. "Yeah, I've got to get out of here, too. I'll walk you to your car."

7

When I am feeling completely overwhelmed, I

- a. just keep putting one foot in front of the other
- b. pile on something else
- c. check into a spa
- d. whine a lot

It took almost half an hour to find my way out to the expressway, since I'd somehow managed to get myself completely turned around when I left the station. Then I crawled along with the bumper-to-bumper traffic for double the time it should have taken me to get home. It was my own fault for hanging around so long talking to David Callahan. I'd have to remember to leave the station earlier from now on.

My stomach was growling, so I rooted around unsuccessfully in the glove compartment for a snack. I thought about pulling my car over to the side of the road to call Jeff, or even making a cautious call while I drove. But cars were driving in the breakdown lane, and I decided I was distracted enough from my driving with worry and starvation, without trying to add dialing and talking to the mix. I looked at the clock on the dashboard. Jeff would have picked up Jackson from soccer practice an hour ago. They'd have stopped for groceries and gone home. Something, probably not something particularly imaginative or nutritious, but something, would be in the oven by now. My stomach growled again in anticipation.

There was no easy way to get home to Rocky Point from the highway. As I wound my way through the tree-lined back roads, I was feeling more exhausted by the minute. I'd already taken off my jacket before I got into the Caravan, but now I unbuttoned the top button of my pants and yanked my T-shirt out until it was completely untucked. I reached down to one knee-high stocking and then the other, pulling them down my calves until they flopped comfortably around my ankles. If I'd had some pajamas in the car, I would have found a way to change into them.

"Oh, good, you're home," Jackson said as I let myself in the kitchen door. "We're starving."

I sniffed the air for the smell of cooking food. Nothing. I dropped my bag on the floor and opened the refrigerator door. Nothing. I closed the door and leaned my head against it. A refrigerator magnet fell to the floor and shattered on the tiles. Plaster of Paris was so unforgiving. I hoped they were using sturdier materials for preschool projects these days.

The first year Olivia was in preschool, she'd made the hot-pink heart magnet for me for Mother's Day. In thick red letters she'd painted MOME, which I'd eventually figured out meant Mommy. At the time I worried about a spelling disability, but over the years the magnet had become a treasure. It was gone now. I slid down to the floor and sat among the pieces of the magnet, staring at my ankles in their billowing black knee highs. Salty tears stung my eyes and slid down my cheeks to the corners of my mouth. I was so hungry that they actually tasted like food.

Jackson slid down to the floor beside me and put his arm carefully around my shoulders. "It's okay, Mom," he said. "I'm not that hungry."

"Hey, what's everybody doing on the floor?" Jeff asked from the doorway. His shoes were off and he had his reading glasses so low on his nose that they looked like they were going to fall onto his mustache.

"Mom forgot the food," Jackson said.

I couldn't help myself. "I did not," I said. "Dad did."

Jeff's eyes met mine and I watched realization hit them. He took off his glasses, shrugged. "Sorry. What can I say? I had a lot on my mind."

Like I didn't. I could feel Jackson waiting for my reaction. I leaned my head against his. "I'm hungry," I said, my eyes still on Jeff's.

Jeff crossed his arms over his chest. "Well, I'm too tired to go out now. Can't we just get some take-out delivered?"

"In case you haven't noticed, we have no milk, no cereal, nothing for Jackson's lunch tomorrow . . ." I gave a martyred sigh and started to get up. "I'll go."

"You guys stay here," Jackson said. "I'll go."

I turned to look at him. "You can't drive," Jeff and I said at the same time.

"I've watched you two do it for years. It looks pretty easy." Jackson shifted his weight forward and stood up without touching the ground with his hands. I remembered when I could do that. He took a couple of steps toward the row of hooks on the back of the kitchen door where we kept the keys.

"Nice try, sport," Jeff said. He bent his head forward and scratched his scalp a few times. He folded the paper he'd been reading, placed it on the kitchen table, and carefully centered his reading glasses on top of it. He yawned extravagantly. "Come on, kiddo, put those sneakers of mine back on those big feet of yours. You better come with me and make sure I don't miss anything."

Jackson's bony elbows stuck out from the sides like wings as he tied his sneakers. He still made two loops with the laces and kind of wrapped them around each other to make a bow. The rest of his fine motor skills seemed perfectly normal, even above average, so I guessed it was a personal choice.

Jeff picked up his wallet from the wicker basket on the kitchen counter he always left it in and slid it into the pocket of his jeans. He took a few steps out into the mudroom and came back with two sweatshirts. I watched, still on the floor, as they both worked their arms through the sleeves first and then, with impeccable timing, flipped the rest of the sweatshirt up in the air, then wiggled their heads out through the hoods. It was an odd sort of male choreography, perfectly synchronized, and for some reason it made me think of watching penguins at the aquarium. Maybe because their movements were at once familiar and totally foreign. I'd never in a million years put on a sweatshirt like that.

I melted. "Okay," I said. "I'll go with you."

●

It was a beautiful night. I hadn't really noticed before. The air was barely cool and had just a hint of the ocean in it. Our house was about a quarter of a mile from the water so the wind and tide had to be just right to smell it, though we joked that if the beach erosion kept up, we'd be waterfront before we knew it. I stood for a moment beside Jeff's Accord, looking up at the sky. I tried to pick out the first star I saw so I could make a wish. I made a decision, focused on my chosen star, and wished that Olivia would be happy at school. Then I added a postscript that it would be nice if things worked out between us at WQBM, too, but made it clear that that was secondary.

As soon as we pulled out of the driveway, Jackson asked from the backseat, "Can Brian and Zack sleep over the day after tomorrow?"

"Not on a school night," I said.

"Mom, the day after tomorrow's Friday. Come on, please? I'll tell them to bring food."

It was worse than I'd thought. I'd barely started the semester and already my daughter hated me, I'd lost track of what day it was, and my son thought his friends had to bribe us with food to stay at our house. I looked over at Jeff, who had gotten me into this mess in the first place. His eyes were on the road and he seemed oblivious. He leaned forward and turned up the radio. WQBM, I noticed. I caught myself listening for David Callahan, not that he'd said anything about being on the air himself, but with that voice of his he should be. Instead, I heard an unfamiliar voice and the staccato play-by-play of some kind of sports game.

I shifted around to look in the backseat. "Jackson, of course they can sleep over. And we'll buy plenty of food. Don't worry, honey."

By the time we walked into Stop & Shop, I had a plan. "Okay, Jackson, get your own cart and you can fill it up with whatever you guys want for Friday night."

"Cool."

"Within reason," I said. Jackson gave me a wide-eyed innocent look and took off toward the middle aisles that carried all the junk food.

"Can I get my own cart, too?" Jeff asked.

"No, you have to share. I'm too tired to push my own."

"Spoilsport." Jeff pulled a cart out and we headed over to the produce section. The store was fairly empty at this hour. There didn't seem to be any other families at all, just a few individual people in work clothes hurrying by with handheld baskets.

I tried to remember how long it had been since Jeff and I had gone to the grocery store together. He pulled two plastic produce bags from a roll and handed one to me. I started filling mine with McIntosh apples, and he stood beside me and began filling his with Granny Smiths. He shifted his body, just slightly, until it was touching mine. I leaned into him.

"Piggly Wiggly," he said.

I shook my head. "Oh my God, I haven't thought about that for so long."

"Remember how every time we saw one in Florida, the kids would crack up and we'd have to go inside even if we didn't need groceries, just so we could get something that said *Piggly Wiggly* on it to take back home with us."

We smiled at each other. "Yeah," I said. "Remember the year

our hotel room had a VCR and we rented movies and got a Piggly Wiggly video rental card, and the kids fought so hard about who got to keep it in their wallet?"

"And we finally went back and got another one in your name so they each could have one."

I leaned over and kissed Jeff on the cheek. "Remember," I said, "when we lived in Cleveland and we used to have to put things back at the grocery store so we'd have enough money to pay?"

Jeff put his hand on my forearm. "I hate to break it to you, honey, but we'd still be doing that if they didn't take charge cards now."

I pushed past him to get to the cart.

He grabbed me by both elbows and pulled me to him. "When was the last time I told you I love you?"

"I don't know," I said, "but I'm so glad you waited for the supermarket." I took his bag of apples from him and placed both bags in the cart. "Jeff," I said.

"Yeah?" He started pushing the cart down the aisle and I put my hands on the bar next to his.

"I love you, too. But I'm not sure going back to school was such a great idea."

He stopped walking. "Really?"

"Yeah, I just feel kind of left out, and I don't think I'll ever get the hang of quantum physics."

"You'll get it. You just have to think really, really small."

I gave the cart a little push. "Easy for you to say."

Jeff pulled the cart back in. "Come on, I'll help you. We'll sit down tomorrow night and I'll break everything down for you into manageable chunks. Once you have a system, you'll be fine."

"Thanks, honey," I said. "But I have two words for you: *stick shift*." Jeff seemed to have temporarily forgotten that, like many couples, we'd learned this important lesson decades ago when Jeff tried to teach me how to drive his car. Our brains are simply not wired the same way and I never got the hang of it. It turned out to be easier, much easier, to sell the car. Over the years, we'd divided everything we had to know down the middle and we each took half. What might have seemed like a means to simplify our lives was really an elaborate way to avoid ever having to try to teach each other anything again.

"Good point," Jeff said.

"And then there's the internship. I'm probably scarring Olivia for life by not quitting."

Jeff steered us over to the lettuce and I reached for the roll of plastic bags. "She'll be fine," he said. "And maybe it'll turn out to be fun."

"How?" I handed him a bag and nodded at the baby spinach.

He picked up the tongs and started adding spinach leaves to his bag. "Yeah, you're right. It'll be hell. And then years from now when we're telling the story, we'll upgrade it to fun."

I concentrated on finding a couple of decent tomatoes. "I don't know. Maybe I should have just kept up the directionality thing. It wasn't that bad."

Jeff finished with the spinach and started picking through the cucumbers. "You know what I've been thinking?" he asked.

"What?" I asked. It was really nice to talk this over with Jeff. He was such a good problem solver, as long as it didn't involve any active teaching on his part.

"I've been thinking about shaving off my mustache."

I stopped. "Where the hell did that come from?"

"I thought we were sharing things."

"I thought you were trying to help me figure out what to do. I thought you were actually listening to me."

Jackson pushed his cart around the corner. "Can we get a toy for Flighty?" he asked. "He's been acting weird. I don't think spending all that time in the garage was very good for him."

8

If you knew then what you know now

o a. you would have been brilliant
o b. you would have had a lot less fun
o c. you still would have made mistakes
o d. you'd never have left your dorm room

Quantum Physics and You had given me a headache. I walked slowly out of the classroom, fishing around in the bottom of my bag for some Advil. A gray-haired woman fell into step beside me. "Wasn't that just divine?" she asked.

"Mmm," I said to be polite. I could just feel a loose tablet. I pulled it out and switched it into my other hand, then dove for another. I hoped they were extra-strength. I stopped walking so I could focus.

"Hello," the same woman said. "I'm Etta Day."

The tablets were covered in gray fuzz. I looked up. "Oh, hi. March Monroe." I couldn't risk losing the Advil by shaking the hand she'd held out to me, so I let my bag slide to the ground so I could shift hands again.

She smiled. "Are you okay, dear?"

"Oh, fine, fine. I just need to take something for a headache." I opened my palm.

Etta leaned down for a look. "Well, those don't seem very promising, but I guess they'll do the trick. Do you need water to take them? I was just headed for the cafeteria for a cup of tea, and I'd love some company."

Water couldn't hurt, I thought, and I was also thinking that I shouldn't turn down my very first on-campus social invitation. "Sure," I said. "But I can't stay long. I don't want to get stuck in traffic." As soon as it came out of my mouth, I regretted it. "Oh, I hope that didn't sound rude," I said, blinking against the headache. "It's just the rush hour traffic is so awful, and I always have a thousand things I should be doing . . ."

She gave my hand, the one that was clutching the Advil, a little squeeze. "Relax, dear. I'll have us both on the road in plenty of time."

We walked along at a pretty good clip, and every once in a while I had to take a little skip to catch up with her. Etta Day had long, powerful legs and a thick head of gamine-styled hair that was really more white than gray. She was wearing a bright pink windbreaker, and the sleeves flapped in the breeze like sails. Etta looked the way I hoped I'd look in twenty or thirty years. Sometimes I actually couldn't wait until I could stop dying my hair, and not care that it would make me look older. I used to think I'd do it at fifty. Now fifty seemed awfully close.

My headache felt better the moment I swallowed my fuzzy

Advil, the same way just the act of pouring a glass of wine or filling the bathtub with hot water sometimes makes me relax. Etta was sipping her tea and telling me why she'd gone back to school. "There are only so many hours in the day you can fill with tennis and painting classes, and one day I realized that I was scheduling my life to make sure I'd be home in time for *General Hospital*."

I took another sip of my water. "I got into the soaps when my daughter was first born. Once she started to talk I was afraid her first full sentence would be, 'Like sand through the hourglass, so are the days of our lives,' so I quit." I hadn't thought about that in years. "Cold turkey," I added, remembering how proud of myself I'd been.

Etta nodded. "Then my husband died, and my world got even smaller. Some days I thought I could literally feel my brain starting to atrophy." She had her hands folded in front of her on the tabletop and I saw that she still wore her wedding and engagement rings. She raised her eyebrows. "So a couple of years ago I decided to be a schoolgirl again."

"How long were you married?"

"Fifty-three years."

"Oh, I'm so sorry." I hoped she knew I meant I was sorry about her husband dying, not about her being married to him for so long. I tried to imagine another thirty-something years with Jeff, what it would be like when he died. "It must be so hard." I turned my own wedding band around on my finger.

Etta took a final sip of her tea and patted her mouth with her napkin. "Well, dear, to tell you the truth, he wasn't much of a husband when he was alive, but he's gotten better every minute since I buried him."

●

After Jeff and Jackson left Friday morning, I fought the urge to crawl back into bed just because I could. Instead, I poured another cup of coffee and reminded myself to prioritize. Directionality coaches are always reminding everyone to prioritize. It's pretty much a requirement.

I had tons of reading to do to stay ahead in my English novel class, a quiz on the Greek gods to study for, and my Quantum Physics and You class was killing me. I was worried it was going to destroy my grade-point average for the semester. I really wanted to learn for the sake of learning, but I also wanted to get at least a 4.0.

I spent most of the morning studying, then headed out for a dentist appointment and to drop off some dry cleaning and get the oil changed in my car. I'd scheduled my session with Ahndrayuh for later in the afternoon because I wanted to make sure her kids were home before I got there. Given that she didn't, as they say, work outside the home, this should have been easier than it was. I wondered if I was feeling judgmental about Ahndrayuh's mothering style, or envious of her ability to take time for herself. Probably a little bit of both, I decided.

I figured the sooner I could teach Ahndrayuh to multitask while her kids were there—maybe make a game out of exercising together, tidying up, or preparing food—the sooner I could get rid of her. I stopped my car behind a school bus that was letting kids off at the end of Ahndrayuh's street. A group of mothers, young and pretty and dressed to be seen by their neighbors, clumped together waiting for their children. I thought I'd have a flash of yearning, but it didn't happen.

What I felt was pure relief that I no longer had to endure the conversations I imagined they were having: whose child got how many A's on her report card, who was picked for what part in the play, who'd made the traveling team in what sport.

A line of grade school–aged kids began filing off the bus. Most of them had oversized drawings and lunch boxes clutched in one hand, while brightly colored backpacks bumped down the steps behind them, dragged by the other hand. Their clothing, which had no doubt been crisp in the morning, had wilted and twisted into something a lot less tidy. God, they were so adorable. I didn't miss the everyday of it, but I missed the sweetness of that time. Olivia and Jackson were just that cute. Probably even cuter.

I glanced back to the group of mothers, trying to pick out Ahndrayuh. A couple of beeps behind me made me jump, and I looked in the rearview mirror. An espresso-colored Suburban hovered over me, dwarfing me even in my minivan. Ahndrayuh was behind the wheel of the Suburban, waving wildly.

A little boy looked up warily, then lifted one hand in a small wave of his own. He started walking toward his mother and her SUV, which must have looked even more frighteningly oversized to him than it did to me. Remembering Ahndrayuh's story about backing over her son's foot with this monster, I checked for signs of a limp as he walked. Fortunately, I didn't see any.

The bus drove away. I rolled down my window, waved to get Ahndrayuh's attention, and gestured for her to go ahead of me. I looked in my rearview to see if she understood, and saw that she was motioning for me to go. She probably didn't want to miscalculate and take a piece of my car with her. I appreciated that.

I drove forward, then turned right into Farm Hills Pathe which, as far as I could see, didn't seem to have even one of the three elements it had been named after. Halfway down the street, I pulled into Ahndrayuh's driveway, leaving her plenty of room beside me.

"You just would not believe the day I've had," Ahndrayuh said, as she pulled Hillary out of her carseat. Clark jumped out on his own, empty-handed.

Automatically, I reached in for his backpack and lunch box. "Hi," I said. "Here you go."

"Thanks," he said. He had a round face, dark hair, Harry Potter glasses. "How did you know those were mine?"

I'd completely forgotten that once upon a time Olivia and Jackson asked questions with answers that were this obvious to adults. I smiled. "I'm a good guesser," I said.

We followed Ahndrayuh and Hillary into the house. "Pick out some snacks while I change," she said to the kids. Maybe to all of us. Hillary and I followed Clark into the kitchen. He pulled the handle of a long, narrow cherry cabinet, and an entire, compact pantry slid out, perfectly accessible. I'd always wanted one of those. The white grid shelves were filled with every prepackaged snack item imaginable. Clark and Hillary considered the possibilities seriously.

The phone rang once then stopped, and I heard the muffled sound of Ahndrayuh laughing upstairs. I looked around the kitchen for something resembling fresh food. A bunch of perfectly ripe bananas dangled from a teak holder. I eyed the contents of the pantry again, and selected a snack-sized box of raisins and a jar of peanut butter.

"Okay, jump up to the counter," I said. "We're going to make bumps on a log." Clark climbed up on one of the tall chrome stools, and I removed the tray from the front of Hillary's high chair, placed it on the ground, and carried the chair across the kitchen to the enormous granite island. I reached down, lifted her up, and put her in the chair. Her fine pale hair smelled like baby shampoo. I held on to her with both of my hands while I used one foot to push the chair snugly under the lip of the counter.

I opened half a dozen cabinets before I found the plates, then pulled out a couple of drawers before I discovered three butter knives. I placed a plate in front of each of us.

"We're not allowed to use knives," Clark said. He placed his two index fingers on the outside edges of his glasses and pushed them farther up his nose.

When Hillary took her thumb out of her mouth, you could hear the small squeak of the suction breaking. "Ouch," she said. She put her thumb back in her mouth.

"We'll be very, very careful and we'll use them very, very safely," I said, thinking if Ahndrayuh wanted to make the rules she'd have to show up first. The kids nodded seriously so I offered them each the handle of a knife. They held the knives out in front of themselves stiffly, as if they were waiting to start a sword fight.

I placed a banana on each of our plates. "Put your knife down first," I said. We peeled our bananas, then picked up our knives again. Placing my hand over theirs on the knives, I helped first Clark and then Hillary cut the bananas in half vertically and place them cut side up on the plate.

I put a big dollop of peanut butter and some raisins on the corner of each of our plates. We slathered the top of the banana halves with peanut butter. Then we made a row of raisins across the top of each one. "Abracadabra please and thank you," I said, just the way I'd said it to Olivia and Jackson. "There you have it, ladies and gentlemen, bumps on a log." I picked up one of mine and took a bite. Milk, I remembered, you need milk with these things.

Hillary picked one of hers up with both hands and bit into the center, dipping her nose into the peanut butter. Clark and I both laughed, and he moved his more carefully to his mouth. Just before it got there he stopped and looked at me. "Can you work here every afternoon?"

Ahndrayuh walked into the kitchen, ignoring us. The next session, I thought, will absolutely be our last one. She was still talking on the phone, not that I felt like letting her in on my newfound pearl of wisdom anyway. But just in case they might remember it one day, I decided to share it with the kids. "Karma is a boomerang," I said in between bites of bumps on a log. "Just you wait and see."

9

The most important thing you can give your
teenager is

○ a. love
○ b. a bigger allowance
○ c. the benefit of your wisdom and experience
○ d. a BMW

As I pulled into my driveway, I could see a small pink-and-white-striped Victoria's Secret bag hooked onto the red flag on the side of the mailbox. I hoped it was underwear—I could use some. Although I supposed underwear didn't often show up on one's mailbox uninvited.

I parked the car and walked over to the mailbox and unhooked the bag. I reached through the tissue paper and pulled out a can of oven cleaner. *Thinking of You, Love, Dana* was written in tiny letters on the plastic top. Smiling and shaking my head, I stuffed the oven cleaner back into the

Victoria's Secret bag, grabbed the mail from the mailbox, and walked inside.

Jackson was sitting at the kitchen table reading my Tampax box. "Hi, honey," I said, taking my time approaching him so he could pretend he hadn't been reading it.

"Hi, Mom," he said without looking up from the box. As I got closer, I realized it wasn't actually the box he was reading. He'd opened the top and unfolded the printed sheet of paper that was always packed inside and was reading that.

"You hungry?" I asked, not sure what else to say. I tried to remember whether I'd put the Tampax box away with the rest of the groceries last night. My standards weren't the highest, especially lately as Dana had so kindly reminded me, but I'd hoped I was still above leaving tampons on the kitchen table.

Jackson looked up from the box. I noticed he'd put his index finger on the paper to hold his place. I also noticed that his fingernails needed to be cut. "Nah," he said. "I'm full. I had some cereal when I got home. Cocoa Puffs."

First things first. Balancing the Cocoa Puffs with something healthier could probably wait until dinner. Mentioning Jackson's fingernails could wait even longer, since no one would really see them until he went back to school on Monday. The Tampax box was definitely top on the list. "Honey," I said, looking at the box, "is there something you still don't understand?"

"About what?"

"About anything. Reproduction. Menstruation. Tampons versus sanitary napkins. Whatever you want to know." As a parent it was so hard to do the sexuality thing right. The scope and sequence of what you were supposed to cover and what the school would cover was never quite clear. You could think you'd done it all, that you'd read your kids all the right books when they were younger, had enough embarrassing talks when they got a little older, strategically left some more books around the house when they were older still. You could hope that school and prime-time television had filled in anything you missed or didn't know yourself. But what if you left some huge gap in their education? Not that Jeff had ever read a Tampax box when I'd met him, but still.

"No, thanks. I'm good," Jackson said, as if I'd asked him whether he wanted another cookie.

I was too curious not to ask. "Is there any particular reason you're reading that box?" I asked brightly.

"Yeah, I'm looking for something to do a science report on."

What an amazingly secure child I'd brought up. "Human reproduction is a great topic," I said.

"No. Toxic shock syndrome."

"Oh. Well, I suppose that's a good one, too." I opened the refrigerator and tried to remember what I'd planned on cooking for dinner.

I looked over my shoulder, figuring I'd move along to the next item on the list since the Tampax mystery had been so easily solved. "Don't forget about your fingernails, honey. The nail clippers are in the medicine cabinet in the upstairs bathroom."

"No they're not. Olivia took them with her."

"Try the other bathroom." I was still noticing stray items that had disappeared along with Olivia. My favorite eyeliner, the local phone book. Not a big deal, just more evidence of her self-absorption, as if there were still some room for doubt in that arena. I couldn't imagine that Olivia had even once stopped to think that she might be taking something someone else might need. Or, I supposed, even that someone else had needs. In a way, I envied her self-centeredness. In another way, it drove me crazy.

"I looked," Jackson said. "There aren't any."

"Well, can you bite them off or something, just this once?" After last night's shopping jaunt, I'd imagined spending the entire weekend at home, maybe even in my pajamas. It would be heaven not to leave the house at all, not to even have to drive a couple of miles down the street to CVS for nail clippers.

"Gee, thanks, Mom. You're encouraging me to take up addictive habits now?"

"Fine, fine. I'll see if I can find an emery board or something."

"Great, why don't you bring me some polish, too, while you're at it."

"Come on, Jackson, give me a break, okay? I'm really tired."

"Sorry, Mom. So, did you have a good day today?"

"Oh, honey, thanks for asking." One of the things I most loved about Jackson was that he never stopped being sweet for long, even when he was working his adolescent attitude a little. "Yeah, it was fine," I said. "How about you? Did you have a good day?"

"Yeah, but my classes all suck."

"Oh well. It's Friday." I turned back to the refrigerator for another look. "So what do you want for dinner?"

"Brian and Zack are sleeping over, remember?"

I'd completely forgotten. "Oh, right. Before or after dinner?"

"I don't know."

I turned back around to face Jackson. He opened the kitchen drawer closest to the stove and took out a pair of full-sized orange-handled scissors. "How are they going to get here?" I asked. "Are they getting dropped off or are we picking up?" If I had to go out, I might as well stop at CVS for nail clippers after all.

"I'm not really sure. They'll probably just show up." Jackson stood over the sink and started to cut his nails with the scissors.

"Jackson! You'll cut off a finger. Sweetie, wait, I'll get you some nail clippers tonight."

"I'm good, Mom. These work fine." Jackson's head and shoulders were hunched forward in concentration.

I watched carefully for signs of bloodshed. "Well," I said finally. "I just need to know what to make for dinner."

"Don't worry about us, Mom. We'll just graze." Jackson put the scissors back in the drawer and started heading off toward his room. He stopped under the archway that led to the family room, and I noticed just how tall he was getting. "Oh, and Mom, Feral is scratching at her ears again. And Flighty laid an egg."

"Flighty's a girl?" I asked.

"She has to be if she laid an egg, Mom."

●

Flighty had literally descended on me one day about a year and a half ago. It was Mother's Day, and the four of us had gone out to the yard to find a place to plant the lacecap hydrangea Jeff and the kids had given me along with breakfast in bed. "I think hydrangeas prefer partial shade so they don't wilt in the sun," I said, wondering if I was confusing them with azaleas.

Jeff nodded. He leaned against the handle of the shovel and looked around the yard for an empty space. Jackson was dribbling a soccer ball on the spongy lawn, and Olivia was checking messages on her hot-pink cell phone.

I was just standing there, enjoying the sunshine and the sweet smell of the viburnum blooming next to the screened porch. And being with my family, even if they were all slightly distracted. It was sort of like the parallel play of toddlers. We were all in the same vicinity, but we were playing next to one another instead of with one another.

Suddenly I saw a flash of white out of the corner of my eye and felt a light pressure on my shoulder. Olivia was the first to notice. "Mom, don't move. There's a bird on your shoulder." She took her cell phone away from her ear and pushed a button.

I froze. "Get it off me," I said as if it were a spider or a wasp. Jackson picked up a small branch and held it in front of my face. The bird stayed where it was. "Jeff," I said, just this side of panic. "Get it off me."

"I don't think we should frighten it," Jeff said.

"Thanks," I said.

"Those orange circles on its cheeks look like makeup," Olivia said. "I bet it's worth a fortune."

"Yeah," Jackson said. "There's probably a huge reward for it. Look, it even has a band on its leg."

I turned my head just a little to try to get a better look. I was starting to get used to having a bird on my shoulder, I noticed. Human beings were so amazingly adaptable. "How do you know it's valuable?" I asked. "Maybe it's just your basic bird."

"I think it's tropical," Jeff said. "Indigenous New England birds aren't white like that."

"What about pigeons?" Olivia said.

"And seagulls," Jackson said. "Sandpipers, terns . . ."

"Okay, okay," Jeff said. "Maybe I meant the orange cheeks, but it sure looks tropical to me."

I tried again to get a good look, and I must have turned my head too far, because the bird flapped its wings in warning. I jumped and it flapped some more. "Okay, that's it," I said. "One of you has to get this bird off me."

Jeff placed the shovel on the ground next to the still-potted hydrangea and took my hand. "Everyone start walking slowly toward the house," he said. "Take your time. Don't anybody make any sudden moves."

I can't believe this is how I'm spending my Mother's Day, I thought as I slowly walked a bird into our house. The bird must have liked being inside since it jumped right off my shoulder and onto the kitchen counter. I guessed it was about a foot long, not that I'd had any experience in estimating the length of birds, and it wasn't technically white, but white with a yellowish cast, and it had two soft round orange circles on its cheeks. The spiky plume on top if its head and the way it strutted manically back and forth across the kitchen counter reminded me of the time Jeff and I had seen Rod Stewart in concert. He'd looked about the same size, too, from the seats we had way at the back of the highest balcony of the old Boston Garden.

Jeff called the local animal shelter and described the bird in precise detail, while the rest of us watched the bird jump to the top of the paddle fan. "Just a minute," he said into the phone. He lowered the phone and asked, "Can anybody read what the band on its foot says?"

Jackson jumped up on a chair and spread his arms for balance. He stood on his tiptoes to get closer to the bird's ankle, and I grabbed the back of the chair so it wouldn't tip. "Oh, neat," he said. "It's the year it was born." His voice changed to babytalk. "Little birdie is just two years old."

Jeff repeated the information into the phone then nodded his head. "You're sure about that?" he asked. "Really? Uh-hmm. Okay, thanks. You have a nice day, too." He hung up the phone and turned to look at us. "A cockatiel," he said. "Not much chance of a reward being posted. Apparently nobody wants a cockatiel. And if they do, they're about fourteen ninety-nine on sale at Wal-Mart." The bird started to whistle and we all looked up at it.

"Oh my God," Olivia said. "That's 'Row, Row, Row Your Boat.'"

"No way," Jackson said. "It's 'Zip-A-Dee-Doo-Dah.'"

"Oh, yeah," Jeff said. "I almost forgot. They said it will probably only live another thirteen years. But maybe as many as eighteen."

"Don't worry, Flighty," Olivia said in a little girl voice. "I'll take very, very good care of you for the rest of your life, no matter what."

Yeah, right, was my first thought. *I know who'll end up being the bird watcher.*

I wasn't far off. To be fair, Olivia occasionally chopped up pieces of apple and shared them with Flighty, and Jackson let Flighty out of the cage to fly around the house on a regular basis, and Jeff taught Flighty to whistle a recognizable version of "Stairway to Heaven." But nine times out of ten, I was the one who had to remind everyone to change the water, add some seed mix or pellets, clean the cage. Either that or do it myself, and sometimes it was just easier to do it myself.

My second thought, the day Flighty flew into our lives, was *eighteen years*? It wasn't that I had anything against birds, or even pets in general. It just seemed to me that whenever you started to see an end in sight, like your kids getting older, for instance, life simply threw you another caretaking curve ball.

•

When Jeff got home from work, Jackson was in the family room showing Brian and Zack Flighty's egg. "Shh," Jeff said, putting his arm around me as we stood in the hallway, out of sight. "This could be good."

I reached my arm around Jeff's waist and we both peeked through the open doorway.

The three boys were gathered around the cage. "Yeah, big deal, it's an egg," Zack said.

"How long till it hatches?" Brian asked.

"It's not fertilized," Jackson said. "So it won't hatch. Poor Flighty, no baby birdie for you."

"So get it a boy bird," Brian said.

"Retard," Zack said. "You have to do it *before* you lay the egg."

"So, they can do it for the next one," Brian said. "Right?"

"Wanna bake a cake?" Jackson asked.

Jeff went over to see Flighty's egg, and I followed the boys out to the kitchen. "You know how to make cake?" Brian was asking Jackson. "I've never made cake."

"Me neither," Zack said. "So what."

I'd never quite understood how Jackson chose his friends. They were always followers, kind of lumpy and bumpy like shapeless hunks of clay waiting to be molded, and Jackson seemed the clear leader. I hoped years of being bossed around by his older sister hadn't destined him to a life of compensation.

I watched Jackson put a cake mix and a frosting can on the kitchen counter, and place two eggs precariously beside them. Then he opened a cabinet, stood on his tiptoes, and reached over his head for a glass mixing bowl. "Need any help?" I asked.

"No, we're good," Jackson said. He cracked the eggs into the bowl, and put the shells on the counter.

I couldn't resist. I grabbed the egg shells and stepped on the lever that opened the trash compactor. An entire plastic army stared up at me from inside an extra-strength freezer bag. "Jackson," I said. "Did you mean to throw away your action figures?" I reached out to them, poised for a quick rescue, with the hand not holding the egg shells.

"Nah, they're not thrown away. We're just trying to make them taller."

Some things you just have to stay out of. I put the egg shells on the counter again and wandered back out to the living room. Jeff looked up. "What do you think, March? Maybe we should take Flighty's egg away so he, I mean she, doesn't get her hopes up. Listen to this, though. I think we've got a pretty good harmony going tonight."

I sat down on the couch and Feral jumped up on my lap and pressed her head against my hand. I scratched her behind the ears the way she liked it as we watched Jeff and Flighty whistle "Stairway to Heaven" for the umpteenth time.

When our kids were younger and taking up every minute of our time, and we had no privacy we could count on, I used to imagine that when they were able to take care of themselves, Jeff and I would date again. All the romance, the newness, the excitement of our first years together, not to mention the sex, would be back.

Here it was, right now, that time in our lives. But instead of sneaking upstairs with my husband for a romantic interlude, a tryst, I was scratching behind a cat's ears while I listened to him whistle in perfect harmony with a bird.

10

Never offer your college freshman

o a. a guilt trip
o b. a home-cooked meal s/he has to come home for
o c. a family vacation during spring break
o d. a bedspread you crocheted

The WQBM receptionist wiggled one bronzed nail at me in what seemed to be a greeting. I smiled and waved, modeling some more welcoming behavior for her, as I walked past her and hurried down the hall. I'd needed to pee since thirty seconds after leaving my house. Staying hydrated made a lot of sense in terms of health and beauty, but not always in terms of comfort. I pushed open the door to the restroom and found Olivia sitting on the none-too-clean tile floor. "Oh, honey, it's okay," I said automatically. I pushed open a stall as quickly as I could and shut it behind me.

"Gee, thanks," she said in a ragged little voice I knew well.

"I'll be right out," I said through the door. By the time your daughter gets to be eighteen, you can pretty much identify high drama on sight. And I really had to pee.

I washed my hands and handed Olivia a cold, wet paper towel. She covered her eyes with it and leaned her head back against the wall. I looked at myself in the mirror, and my reflection and I both raised our eyebrows.

I waited until Olivia removed the paper towel from her face and looked up. She twisted a corner of the towel and wiped at the streaks of black mascara running down from her eyes.

"Do you want to talk about it?" I asked. To give her some space, I turned and examined my face in the vast expanse of mirrors over the sinks. Not a good move. I could convince myself that I was aging well until I ran into a harsh fluorescent light.

I looked over at Olivia. I was relieved to see the light wasn't doing much for her face, either. So that meant that I didn't really look half as bad as I seemed to. Dropping her head down to rest on her knees, Olivia let out a long sigh. "I. Hate. My. Room. Mate," she said in a muffled voice, taking a histrionic breath between each word.

"Oh, honey," I said.

"My. Room. Mate. Is. A. Psy. Cho. Path," Olivia continued. I watched her carefully for a minute just in case she started to hyperventilate from all that extra air.

"What did she do?" I asked in a calm, measured voice, while I sneaked a look at my watch. I knew these things took time, but I also didn't want us to be late for the intern meeting.

Olivia sat up straight and blew her nose on her paper towel, then folded the ends over and crunched it into a ball. She executed a perfect toss into the beige metal wastebasket. She rubbed her hands together a few times, and when she spoke she had her normal voice back. "What doesn't she do? She goes out and leaves the door open on me when I'm sleeping."

"Oh, that's awful," I said. "Not to mention dangerous."

"And," Olivia continued, rubbing her hands back and forth on the thighs of her jeans, "she cuts her toenails in our sink and leaves them there."

It would have been such a perfect segue, but I figured this probably wasn't the best time to bring up the fact that she'd absconded with all our nail clippers. I'd read an article recently about how a huge number of college freshmen were having roommate problems. Apparently this was the first generation to grow up without sharing a bedroom, so they were completely unprepared for the give and take living with another person requires. And now the colleges were scrambling to build more single dorm rooms to accommodate the spoiled children my generation had raised. There truly was no end to parental guilt. "Try telling her she's disgusting and make her clean up the toenails. That always works with Jackson. And Dad."

"No, you don't get it," Olivia said. "When I tell her to clean them up she just says they're not her toenails. And she walks around naked all the time, which is like totally sick, especially since we're not even speaking to each other, and she uses my razor. And she eats my Nutri-Grain bars. And she cooks fat-free hot dogs in my microwave. I mean, I'm the one who brought the microwave. I don't trash her iron. I hardly even touch it."

"Fat-free hot dogs?" I said.

"Like they're really fat-free." Olivia shook her head. "I know the sound of fat sizzling."

"Well, she should be careful. Hot dogs can explode all over the microwave."

"That's what happens," she said. "They explode all over the

microwave and now I can't use it because everything tastes like hot dog."

"Try washing it really well, then scrub it with baking soda."

"Why should I wash it? I didn't cook hot dogs in it."

I sneaked another peek at my watch. "That's tough," I said. "Do you think you should go right over to Student Housing and request a new roommate?"

"I did," Olivia said, and I noticed her breathing was getting shallow again. "They said. All the rooms. Are. Full." I watched her lower lip start to quiver.

I slid down to the floor beside her. "I had a horrible roommate freshman year," I said. Olivia dropped her head back down to her knees. "Well, actually, she was okay, but her boyfriend came to visit every weekend and I used to have to pretend to be asleep so they wouldn't think I heard the springs creaking on her side of the room."

Olivia's head shot up. "Oh my God. People did that back then?"

I decided to ignore the implication that I'd been born in the presexual era. "So, the next year I got a new roommate and she turned out to be bulimic, although we didn't have a name for it back then. We called it wanting to be an actress."

Olivia rested her head lightly against my shoulder. "What happened?"

"To the roommate? I think she switched her major from drama to marketing and stopped vomiting. And then I met Dad, and I started spending my time with him, and so the rest of it didn't matter as much." I thought it best to leave out the part about sleeping over at his house.

"Wow, you were practically my age when you met Dad, weren't you?"

"A little older."

"Do you ever wonder who you would have met if you hadn't met him?"

I tilted my head until it touched the top of Olivia's. "Well, sometimes I wish I'd met him just a few years later. It probably would have been better to finish college back then."

"But then you might have missed Dad."

"That's true." I slid my arm around her shoulder. "Honey," I said. "I'm really sorry you're having such a tough time. Maybe you should come home for a night or two. A break from it all might do you some good."

Olivia was on her feet in less than a second. "God, it's not like *that* bad," she said, checking her face in the mirror.

●

It was as if the bathroom were a television show that was playing on a different channel than the one in the kitchen. When I joined Olivia there, she didn't even appear to recognize me. So I'd occupied myself by trying to figure out who George Dickerman, the person we were waiting for to show up and start the intern meeting, reminded me of. Suddenly it came to me. "Doesn't he remind you of Dabney Coleman in *9 to 5*?" I asked the other interns.

"Is that a band?" Caitlin asked.

"No," I said. "A movie. Dabney Coleman was the boss. He was awful, a complete chauvinist."

"Everything," Olivia said, as she checked a section of her hair for split ends, "reminds her of something from before we were born."

I tried to remember if Jeff and I had had to get a baby-sitter when we saw *9 to 5* or if we'd still been able to waltz right out the door, childless, without a care in the world. I could place a lot of movies that way. We saw *The Breakfast Club* when Olivia was a couple of days old. Jeff wore her in a pink-and-white pin-striped front pack called a Snugli and she slept through the whole movie. I should have enjoyed the whole experience more but I didn't know then that we would never have another peaceful movie for the rest of our lives. For years we'd either have to leave the kids at home and worry about how they were doing with the baby-sitter, or bring them with us and spend the whole movie mopping up spilled soda and taking turns making trips to the bathroom.

Then, later, we'd be able to leave them home alone but we'd have to worry about them burning down the house or having a wild party. And still later, as in right now, I'd be stuck with this nagging worry that what if Olivia's roommate problem really was serious. I guess I'd imagined that a little space would make things easier. Now I thought that *I hope she's okay* would always be just below the surface for me, wherever I was, whatever I was doing, for the rest of my natural life.

I tried not to glare at my daughter, but I felt a quick flash of anger at her complete disregard for the impact she'd had on my life.

"*9 to 5* was a TV show, too," Justin said.

"No, I don't think so," I said. "I think it was just a movie. Lily Tomlin, Jane Fonda, Dolly Parton."

"I thought Dolly Parton was in a band," Caitlin said.

"Dude," Justin said. "I know this one. First it was a movie in like 1980 . . ."

"See," Olivia said. "I told you. We weren't even born."

Justin tilted his chair back again and closed his eyes. I got ready to catch him if he needed it. "Then," he said, "it ran as a TV show for one season in 1982 and then it resurfaced in 1986 in first-run syndication. The theme song was sung by Phoebe Snow in 1982 and later by Dolly Parton."

"Oh my God," I said. "That's amazing."

"One of Justin's majors is entertainment trivia," Caitlin said.

"You can major in that?" I asked.

"Dude. At my school you can major in anything."

11

Your greatest strengths

○ a. are your natural talents

○ b. may have atrophied slightly

○ c. are around here somewhere

○ d. depend on how often you go to the gym

The receptionist pushed open the kitchen door to let us know that all four interns were supposed to sit in on *Karyn's Karmic Korner*. She looked down at the note she held pinched between two of her shiny bronze talons, and added, "Apparently she needs more faces for today's show." She looked up. "If you ask me, she could use a couple more pounds on her for it, too."

I was the only one to laugh politely. She ignored me. "Immediately afterward," she continued, "give or take, you'll meet with His Highness back in here." She crumpled the note into a ball and dropped it into the big plastic trash barrel that sat in the corner of the kitchen. "That's it."

I followed the other interns through the maze of narrow hallways and into the conference room. The same foam-covered microphones were sitting on the same long, wood-grained table. This time, I knew that David Callahan was sitting in the dark behind the plate-glass window. Just in case he was looking, I gave him a tiny wave. Four empty chairs were spaced evenly on one side of the table, so I headed for the farthest one. When I looked up again, a whiteboard had appeared in the window. *Hi,* it said.

I forgot where the table was until my hipbone hit it. The jolt of pain made my eyes water. I stepped back and got my foot tangled up in the chair somehow and flipped it over backward. "What is your problem?" Olivia whispered as if I had done it just to embarrass her.

While Justin helped me pick up my chair, I glared at her. "Thank you so much for your concern, honey."

"People," Karyn said, "you're destroying the vibrations."

"Are you okay, March?" David Callahan's voice said over the microphone. I jumped, then tried to cover it up with another little wave.

"How does he know your name?" Olivia asked. "Mom, sit down."

A small wooden box sat on the table in front of each chair. A rectangle of screen was inserted into the top of each box, just like the bug boxes that Olivia and Jackson had tried to catch butterflies and ladybugs in when they were little. Usually the boxes ended up holding worms or potato bugs instead, and sometimes just dirt. I looked over at Olivia to see if she remembered, but she had forgotten all about me and was whispering something to Caitlin, who was giggling appreciatively.

"Shh," Karyn hissed from the other side of the table. She was wearing a dress that, in terms of both style and size, looked exactly like a white, billowy parachute. "No more words unless I signal you. And don't play with the boxes. Just leave them on the table until I tell you to touch them. Any questions?"

"Ten seconds," David Callahan's voice said. He had such a great voice.

"Greetings, and welcome to *Karyn's Karmic Corner*. Today I'm going to empower you to create a thoughtform and infuse it with emotional energy."

Huh? I thought. My hip might hurt too much to follow that one. I tried to sneak a peek at the other interns' faces, but I couldn't really see them from where I was sitting. Then I tried to slide my chair just enough to change my angle. It squeaked and Karyn flashed me a disapproving look.

"For the first time on this radio station, and probably any other, we will create what is known as a familiar, also commonly known as an artificial elemental, whose purpose, depending on your particular needs and aura, and the energy circling around all of that, is to serve as your guard, your messenger, or your companion."

It sounded like an imaginary friend to me. I managed to turn my head enough to see Caitlin, who was sitting next to me. She had made her index fingers into a cross, which she held casually out in front of herself at table level. Karyn didn't appear to notice. She reached inside the parachute and pulled a yellowed bra strap back up on her shoulder. Then she leaned into the microphone, lowered her voice, and said, "Warning! Warning! This is your warning, people. Do not create an artificial element, aka a familiar, unless you're willing to accept the seriousness of your actions. It is just as much of a responsibility as owning any other creature, particularly a genie, but also a cat or a dog. And now a word from our local sponsors."

It was hard to know quite what to say. The other interns and I just kind of sat there while Karyn buried her face in her arms to wait out the commercials. I looked up at the darkened window and gave a little smile. "Dude," Justin said finally. "I'm way into this. I'm like totally ready to commit."

"Ten seconds," David's voice said again.

"This is *Karyn's Karmic Korner* and we're back. Okay, unless you're listening to the radio while you're driving your car, I want you to close your eyes. Okay, now visualize a ball of light. Wait a minute. Back up. First I have to tell you how to choose your color and animal. All right, this should probably be two shows but I think we can do it. First, you have to pick earth, air, wind, or fire. If you want your familiar to be healing, that would probably be earth and the ball of light would be brown or green in the shape of a cow or a mouse, maybe. And if you need a familiar to protect you, I'd suggest fire, which would be red or orange, maybe a dragon or a snake.

"Okay, I can give you more details later if you need them but, okay, so you're closing your eyes and picturing a ball of light in the shape of an animal. Which means your familiar has been created, because as soon as you can sense it, it's there. Very important: as soon as you can sense it, it exists.

"You should begin immediately to communicate with your familiar telepathically. You must say, in your mind only, without even moving your lips, 'Greetings, I hereby name you insert name here.' You must use the first name that comes to your mind. Then you must tell it silently why you created it and what its purpose is. Did you create it to stand guard over you? To pass on a message psychically to someone? Communication, as in all relationships, is key here. And now, another word from our sponsors.

"Okay, we have to move fast." Karyn picked up one of the small boxes on the table in front of us. "Pick up your boxes."

"Why?" Caitlin asked.

"Come on, just do it. Now, I'm going to teach everyone how to make homes for their familiars and then I'll ask a couple of you to describe your familiars. We'll see how the time goes. Just be ready."

"What's the screen for?" Olivia asked. She was holding her box in her open palm as if she were afraid of breaking it.

"Those are airholes so it can breathe," Karyn said.

"Ten seconds."

"And this is *Karyn's Karmic Corner* again. If you're just tuning in, we've just had the amazing experience of creating our own familiars, and now we're going to make homes for them. Okay, find an empty box. Here in the studio we have small wooden boxes with screen inserts at the top to allow for breathing, but you can use whatever's handy. An empty chocolate box or a shoe box works well. Okay, cover the box with some beautiful paper, being careful to block off any big escape holes, and draw the symbol of whatever element you've used. Oops, I haven't really explained the symbols but you can just draw a picture of it or write its name. Now, signal your familiar telepathically to use the space you've created for it and to think of it as home."

Karyn leaned in close to the microphone again. "Warning! Warning! Before we hear about some of the familiars created live today by members of our studio audience, let me make it perfectly clear that, once created, you cannot simply abandon your familiar like an old shoe when you're through with it. You must reverse the process you used to create it: first, visualize your familiar, then watch it become an ordinary ball of the appropriately colored light again, and then draw that energy back into yourself by simply inhaling deeply through both nostrils.

"Okay, I think we've got just enough time to hear from a member of the audience. I know you've all been waiting for this. Who wants to describe his or her familiar to our listeners at home?" Justin was waving his hand. "Young man in the front?"

"Dude. Well, I made my familiar from a ball of blue light, so I guess that was air or maybe water. She came out looking like a genie, so I call her Jeannie, after the television show *I Dream of Jeannie*—that was NBC, 1965 to 1970. I guess I could have called her Barbara after Barbara Eden, who played Jeannie through all five years the show ran, but you said to use the first name that came to mind. Anyway, she's probably not going to want to stay in this box, but I'll find her a bottle as soon as I . . ."

Karyn was making cutting motions across her throat. "How about you, way back there in the last row?" she said to Caitlin.

"Sorry," Caitlin said. "I sniffed mine back in. It was completely freaking me out."

The sound of temple bells began filling the room. "Okay, that's all we have time for today on *Karyn's Karmic Korner*. Until next time, just remember . . . karma is a boomerang."

The other interns practically ran out of the conference room as soon as the show was over. I took my time. I wondered if I should knock on the door to the studio and say hi to David. Just to be friendly, and to thank him for his concern about my hip. Or maybe I shouldn't remind him about my hip. It hadn't been one of my more graceful moves.

Olivia jogged a few steps back to me and held out her wooden box. "Hey, Mom, can you give this to Jackson when you get home?"

"Sure, honey. That's really sweet." I smiled. "And who should I tell him is in here?"

Somehow that managed to trigger a dirty look from Olivia. "Just give him the box, okay? He might want to put some bugs in it or something."

David poked his head out the door just as I was hovering in front of it, trying to figure out what I'd said wrong to Olivia. "Oh. March," he said. "I was on my way to find you. Do you need some ice or anything?"

12

In order to get what you want, you have to

o a. take out a loan
o b. wait for your kids to grow up
o c. stop making excuses
o d. figure out what it is

David Callahan was wearing jeans. His hair curled over the collar of a dark denim shirt that matched his eyes. "So," he said, "how'd you like to be a star?"

There didn't seem to be anything in the hallway, but I managed to trip anyway. I put one hand down to break my fall, something I warned my clients never to do because it was a good way to break a wrist or an elbow. Fortunately, all I injured was my remaining self-esteem, which wasn't all that appreciable at that point anyway.

David grabbed the hand that wasn't on the floor and helped me up. "Are you okay?" he asked.

"Fine, fine. Sorry, I'm not usually quite this clutzy. Um, what were you saying?" I leaned back against the wall so I couldn't go anywhere.

"I have an idea for a show. Well, first . . ." He lowered his voice and pointed. "Looney Tunes in there is leaving. She's going back to school." David smiled and I watched his eyes crinkle. "Guess what she wants to be?"

"An energy healer?"

"No, a paralegal. Anyway, I'm pretty sure I can get Dickerman to carry the first month or two if it involves interns and local programming, since he needs both to keep his license. And I don't think it's ever been done before, so I think there's a good chance for syndication. Well, okay, here's the pitch. You and your daughter. A call-in show, wildly divergent opinions on just about everything, maybe with an emphasis on issues surrounding the college scene at any age."

Not only was I tripping all over the place, but now I had to be hearing things. "Excuse me, but did you say my daughter and me?"

●

While David went to get his notes, I made my way back to the kitchen without tripping once. I stood for a moment, one hand on the doorknob, listening to Olivia. "I just told him," she was saying, "you might get away with that with stupid girls but don't try it with me." Caitlin burst out laughing and Justin drummed his response on the tabletop.

A heavy hand landed on my shoulder and I jumped. "I won't tell if you don't," George Dickerman's voice whispered in my ear. "Anything good going on in there?"

He had a lot to learn about respecting personal space. It was all I could do not to say *yuck*. Or *ick*. Or *oh, gross,* the way I would have back in high school. Mature grown-up that I was, I merely turned the doorknob and slid my shoulder out from under Dickerman's beefy paw and walked into the kitchen.

"Hi," I said to the other interns. They looked at me blankly.

Dickerman swung a chair around backward and straddled it. "Let's get right down to it," he bellowed. "No time for chitchat, even the good stuff. Right, Margie?"

"That's Marchie," Justin said. "Quite right, quite right," he added, his British accent appearing from nowhere. Caitlin started to giggle. Olivia looked straight ahead.

David knocked and opened the door. "George," he said. "You were right about all of it." He held one hand up to block his face from Dickerman, and gave the other interns an exaggerated wink. The way he did it made me think he was probably a great dad.

George Dickerman ran his fingers through some strands of hair. He started above one ear, went over the top of his head, and ended up over the other ear. I looked away. "Of course I was," he said. "Which all of it was that?"

David sat down in the seat across from him and laced his fingers behind his head. "I understand Rhonda, aka Karyn, has given her notice, just like you thought she would. So you're absolutely right that you're going to need some more local programming around here unless you want the FCC gunning for your license."

Dickerman pounded the tabletop. "Damn feds. Always trying to get a piece of me. Let that be a lesson to you kids." The kids stared straight ahead. He leaned over the table toward David. "So which plan was it that you liked?"

David unlaced his fingers and rested his forearms on the table. "Remember? The mother-daughter call-in show? You were going to think the format through?"

"Uh, right. Okay, you," Dickerman said, pointing to Olivia, "and your mother here." He nodded vaguely in my direction. He pounded his fist on the table again. "So, what's it gonna be, gals?" He held up four sausagelike fingers to make two sets of quotation marks. *"Howard Stern Lite? Imus in the Early Afternoon?"*

I looked at Olivia and raised my eyebrows, hoping I was signaling to her, *Don't look at me. They weren't my suggestions.*

Olivia cleared her throat. She flipped her hair back away from her face. "What if it's a show about fashion?" she asked, as if this wasn't the first she'd heard of it. As if she'd been thinking about us doing a show all along. "About like what's hot to wear on campus. And what's not. Everyone would tune in to listen. Wouldn't you listen, Caitlin?"

"Definitely. I'd make everyone in my dorm listen, too."

Justin drummed the table. "Dude. Great idea. Hot girls and what they wear would rock."

Dickerman tilted forward in his chair and leered disgustingly. "Hot or cold, you don't have to talk me into the girl part. Okay, let's think this through. Now how would Mama Bear fit in?"

Olivia looked right at me. "Okay, there are probably lots of women your age at home with nothing to do but listen to the radio. You could do the part for them. What to wear when you go out for your anniversary or other special occasions." She looked at my outfit doubtfully. "And we could invite famous fashion people to come on as our guests and they'd give us expensive clothes just so we'd wear them on the show and, well, everywhere. They'd probably even let us keep some of them."

I spoke gently. "Olivia, it's a radio show. The audience won't be able to see the clothes."

She flashed me a laserlike glare. "So? We can describe them."

I tried to keep my tone light. "It's a really interesting idea, but don't you think it might be better if . . ."

"Oh, that's right." She crossed her arms over her chest and looked up at the ceiling. "I completely forgot you know everything. Sorry I tried to have an idea."

As much as I attempted to block out the other three people in the room, I imagined them looking at me, then Olivia, then back at me again as if they were watching a Ping-Pong game. "Olivia," I hedged, "I didn't say it was a bad idea."

"You didn't have to. Your tone is all over the place."

"What's that supposed to mean?"

Justin started a long drum roll. I was happy for the distraction but Olivia whipped her head around to face him. "Shut up, Justin. If you don't mind, I'm trying to tell my mother she's completely ruining my life, all because she has to be right about everything."

"See what I mean," David said. "It's a gold mine."

I gave him a dirty look. I had no problem with his manipulating a creep like Dickerman, but I had no intention of going along for a ride I didn't want to take. It was also really hitting me that I must have made a major parenting mistake during one of Olivia's significant developmental stages. How else could she have turned out this way? I tried to make it into a joke, just as a cover so I could get out of the room and away from all of them. "I'm rubber, you're glue," I chanted at her, which seemed appropriate since the conversation had sunk to about a preschool level, "everything you say bounces off me and sticks to you."

Olivia blew air out of her mouth in a perfect sound of disgust.

Dickerman pounded his fist on the table. "Way to go, Marge. *I'm Rubber, You're Glue,* they're gonna love it. We'll have the audience call in questions and you two can bounce back whatever the hell comes into your minds. They wanna talk about clothes, they'll ask you about clothes. They wanna talk about something else, you can do that, too."

"You're the man, George," David said. He slid his chair back and stood up. "Let's go draw up the details in your office." Dickerman unstraddled his chair and walked out. David followed, but stopped at the kitchen door to give us a thumbs-up. I hoped he could tell I was glaring at him.

"How does this station make any money?" I asked when they were gone.

"It's not like supposed to make money," Caitlin said.

"It's not?" I asked.

"Dude," Justin said. "Dickerman Pharmaceuticals? Mommy and Daddy let their little Dick Man run the BM into the ground as a tax write off. He's been like making them proud for years."

Olivia stood up. "I have a test to study for," she said.

Caitlin stood up, too. "I'll walk with you."

Justin rocked his chair back and forth, then jumped up. "Yeah, I'm outta here. Nobody will bother to check on us again."

I sat at the kitchen table feeling sorry for myself. I replayed the conversation but, other than not saying no to David about the show, and opening my mouth to speak in front of Olivia, I couldn't really see where I'd taken a wrong turn. The door opened just enough for Olivia to stick her head in. "I know you really don't want to do this show," she said, "but I hope just once you won't have to ruin things for me." Just before she slammed the door, she added, "And, by the way, I just want you to know . . ." She paused to let the suspense build. "I'm going to be so rich and famous someday you're going to wish you were nicer to me."

•

There was a small bag of kitty litter on my back porch with a big red bow stuck on the top. I'd really have to give Dana a call one of these days. I let myself in and Feral meowed and pushed up against my ankles. "For you," I said, placing the bag on the floor beside her. "And don't let me catch you putting any more of that in the oven. You've embarrassed me enough as it is."

I walked to the bottom of the stairs and yelled up to Jackson, on the off chance that he might be able to hear me over his after-school computer game. No such luck. Rather than head up the stairs empty-handed, I circled back to the kitchen and put together a plate of cheese and crackers, sliced apple, and baby carrots. I'd learned early that if you cut up healthy food and place it in front of your children without comment during the low-blood-sugar hours of the late afternoon, they will eventually eat it. If you ask first, they will hold out for cookies. At least one of my children would still let me feed him.

I knocked on Jackson's door. "Hey, sweetie," I said when he finally answered my knock. "How was school?"

"Okay." Jackson stared at me as if trying to remember who I

was. I looked back at him, feeling a bit of the same confusion. I'd expected him to be younger somehow. The sad truth was that Jackson had been pretty much moved into his room for about a year now, an event linked in my mind to the day he and his dad went shopping for his first razor. He might be smiling pleasantly, but he didn't really live in the rest of the house anymore. Before I knew it he'd be treating me the way his sister did.

I handed him the plate and he said thanks in that automatic way of kids who were well-drilled at a younger age. "Anything new?" I asked, thinking I should talk to him while I still could.

"Not really."

"Did anything interesting happen at school?"

"Nope."

"Nothing at all?"

"Nada."

"Oh, how was Spanish today?"

"Mom."

"Sorry. Okay, honey. Well, I love you."

"Love you, too. Bye."

I told Jeff and Jackson about the show at dinner. Jackson was pouring milk for everybody and Jeff was slicing the roast chicken. "Guess what?" I said. "Olivia and I are going to have our own radio show."

Jeff speared a piece of chicken. "Together?"

"That's the plan."

Jeff was waving the chicken slice like a flag. "What kind of show?"

I held my plate out to catch it. "A mother-daughter show of some sort. Beyond that, I don't think anybody knows yet."

Jeff remembered the chicken and brought it in for a landing on my plate. "She actually wants to do this show with you?"

I sighed. "Apparently so. I'm pretty sure she thinks I don't want to do it, which means, of course, that she does."

"Wow," Jackson said. "WMOM and WSIS on the same show. That's going to melt a few radios."

13

Statistically, the grades of younger students
are lower than those of returning students
because

o a. they're not paying the bills
o b. they have more fun
o c. they have more sex
o d. they have more fun and sex

Zebra-Thong Girl was late again for The English Novel Before 1800 and, once more, Dr. Nord motioned her to the seat in front of me. She was, true to her name, wearing another thong today, but she'd broadened her repertoire and this one was more cougar than zebra. I wondered if she could feel a draft. I tried to remember if my jeans used to ride down in the back like that in the days when low-rise jeans were called hip-huggers.

The difference was we wore them over a leotard, which we climbed into from the neck hole, either that or with a body stocking that pulled over the head and snapped at the crotch. I always suspected that the bravest girls didn't wear underwear at all with these garments. But my friends and I just rolled the elastic waistband of our highwaisted white cotton underpants down four or five times until their telltale lines were hidden under the heavier fabric of our jeans. Actually, we didn't call them jeans but dungarees and, to be really cool, we wore shawls draped across our shoulders, plus black ballet slippers with no socks and big dangly earrings to complete our look.

I pondered whether I should try a pair of thong underwear once before I died. A thong, I corrected myself. I wondered if wearing one felt like having a permanent wedgie. Or if it was like being naked, only sexier. Olivia had a drawer full of them, just as Jackson had been wearing boxers since the age of eleven or twelve, while Jeff still bought three-packs of Fruit of the Loom briefs and wore them until the elastic gave out. How had it happened that our kids owned better underwear than we did? It didn't seem like a good sign.

The professor was going on and on about Henry Fielding's *Shamela.* I understood that he wanted us to think it was far superior to Samuel Richardson's *Pamela,* which it lampooned for its pretentiousness and excessive morality. I'd actually liked *Pamela,* and I thought *Shamela* was petty and mean-spirited, but I knew enough to nod in all the right places and make eye contact when the professor glanced my way. In terms of social intelligence, I was a much better student this time around.

The women sitting on either side of me were about my age. We were all nodding our heads rather manically and writing away, as if we could make up for all the years we had missed. I managed a quick break by dropping my pen on the floor, accidentally on purpose. It was funny how those little tricks came back to you. When I leaned down to pick it up, I took a peek at the younger students scattered throughout the back rows. Most of them had open notebooks in front of them, but I didn't see anybody actually writing anything. A couple of them even looked like they might be sleeping.

Finally, the class ended. I found myself walking along with Zebra-Thong Girl, escaping the dank air of the basement-level classroom into the crisp October day. Maybe she wasn't so bad after all. "So which one did you like better?" I asked.

She had her cell phone out already. "Which one what?" she asked as she pushed a couple of buttons.

"*Pamela* or *Shamela*—which one did you enjoy reading the most?"

"You actually read them? Hasn't anyone told you about get-thenotes.com yet?" She shook her head and walked faster.

Maybe I was old-fashioned, but I liked to read. Which was a good thing, because it certainly didn't look like I was heading in the direction of a big on-campus social life. I looked around at the other people walking to their next class. The ones my age all seemed to be preoccupied, as if they'd brought their own worlds with them to school. I wandered over to the dining hall and bought a sandwich and a spring water. I carried them outside to eat alone.

●

Etta Day was still my only friend at school. My favorite thing about her, besides the fact that she was the one person at Olde Colony who seemed to like me, was that she mentioned her age a lot, but she always said a different number. I'd noticed there was a range, though. So, unless she'd made them all up, Etta was somewhere between the ages of seventy-eight and eighty-two.

We were sitting in the dining hall having the après Quantum Physics and You cup of tea that was becoming our ritual. I'd just finished telling her about the three dozen things I should have been doing instead of sitting there, and I was starting to feel guilty about monopolizing the conversation. "So how about your sister, Martha," I asked. "Did you talk to her this week?"

"Well," Etta said, "if you call listening to her whine a conversation. 'Martha,' I said to her, 'I don't want to hear about your constipation. Get out there and shake yourself up a little bit. A good long walk is better than a bowl of bran flakes.' I just can't believe that woman is two years younger than I am. It's a disgrace the kind of shape she's let herself get into."

"So what did Martha say to that?" I asked.

"Oh, please." Etta pushed the sleeves of her sweatshirt up over her elbows. "Who listens to what Martha says about anything?" She pulled an envelope out of her backpack and dumped a pile of brightly colored brochures on the table. Etta was planning her next trip and had a new batch every time I saw her. I reached for a handful and started looking through them. "Oh. Oh. I forgot. So then Martha tells me her doctor wants her to lose twenty pounds. And then do you know what she says?"

"What?"

"She says when she was in good shape she didn't have the energy to lose five pounds. So how is she going to lose twenty now?"

I laughed. "Well, maybe she should take a few lessons from

you. I'm sure people tell you this all the time, but you are the absolute picture of health."

"Thanks. I feel like a million bucks. When you get to be my age, March, you've got to take each day as the gift that it is. All right, enough about me. Is that daughter of yours still driving you crazy at the radio station?"

"Crazier by the second." I took a deep breath, ready to launch into the story of Olivia and me getting our own show.

"Kids," Etta said before I could get a new sentence started. "It's a good thing they're so adorable as babies, given all the hoops they make us jump through when they get older. We never quite lose those old memories, and I do believe that's what carries us through the bullshit years."

"How long do the bullshit years last?" I asked, hoping it wouldn't be much longer.

"My son, Edward, is fifty-three."

I laughed.

"The good news, though, is that his own daughter is a little hellion."

"Karma is a boomerang."

"Wisely said, March, wisely said."

I felt a pinprick of guilt about getting credit for Karyn's line. "Well, it's not really original."

"Honey, by the time you get to be my age you'll realize it's all been said before." Etta adjusted the pink bandanna she'd rolled up and tied around her short white hair for a head-band. The knot rested on top of her head, and the two ends stuck out on either side like a small propeller.

A brightly colored sunset made me pick up a brochure about Rio de Janeiro. I'd always wanted to go to Rio. Fat chance. By the time we'd paid off everybody's college bills, I'd be too tired to travel. But I could see Etta in Rio, dancing on the beach during Carnivale. I handed the brochure to Etta. "Do you remember how long it took you to get used to Edward going away to college?" I asked.

Etta looked up at the ceiling as if it were papered with a lifetime's worth of calendars. "Let me see, dear. When Edward went off to Yale, I distinctly remember that every day for a week I went into his room, sat on his bed, and cried." She lowered her head and looked at me. "Then he came home at Thanksgiving. He was out every night until all hours. That was it, I was over him."

She shrugged and picked up an Alaska cruise brochure and started folding the corners in toward the center. The skin on her hands was thin and wrinkled, and dotted with freckles. Actually, they were probably age spots, but Etta wore them like freckles.

I picked up what looked like a stapled together print-out from an online site about a trip to New Zealand. "Oh, this one looks good," I said, holding it out to Etta.

Etta tossed the pages back on the table. "That," she said, "was a suggestion from my just-mentioned son, Edward. It's not even in the running."

I picked it up again. "Why not? I thought you'd always wanted to try New Zealand."

"With Elder Hostel? Not my style at all, I'm afraid. You see the point is to be the only spunky old woman in the group, not to lose myself in a veritable sea of spunky old women."

I reached down and pulled the navy binder out of my bag and placed it on the table. I pulled the test Etta and I had just gotten back out of my binder and took another painful look.

I'd completely blown the question on Heisenberg's Uncertainty Relation. I knew it was something about needing light or another radiation to measure the position and speed of a certain particle. And something about if you have a long wavelength the position is exact but the speed isn't, and with a short wavelength, something else happens. Apparently I was the one on the wrong wavelength for that to make any sense at all. My brain just isn't wired for this stuff.

I read my answer again. I thought I should have gotten at least partial credit for saying that in quantum physics there are never certainties, only probabilities, and that I agreed with Heisenberg and felt that the same thing was true of life in general. Nothing is ever really certain. I still couldn't really see what was wrong with that answer.

"Etta?" I asked. "Do you have time to help me with quantum physics?"

14

The best excuse for why you haven't lived the
life you wanted to is

- a. your kids
- b. yourself
- c. procrastination
- d. short-term memory loss

I made sure I got to WQBM early so I could talk to David
Callahan. "So, tell me one thing," I asked, just the way I'd
practiced it in my head on the drive there. "Exactly why do
you want to do this show?"

He swiveled around in his chair and shut the case on a CD.
"I believe the accepted custom is to say hello before asking
probing questions."

I could feel my face getting warm, either a blush or that first
hot flash I was always half waiting for. It was odd that once
your kids got old enough that you finally stopped worrying

about their temperatures, you started thinking about your own again.

I realized I hadn't said anything back to David. "Hi," was all I managed to come up with. I thought for a moment. "Sorry," I added.

He smiled, and while I didn't exactly feel my knees start to buckle, I could relate to the expression. He was wearing jeans and a soft denim and navy pin-striped shirt, cuffs rolled, collar opened. Blue stripes matching those blue eyes I couldn't seem to stop noticing. Faint smell of something spicy, maybe sandalwood. I knew I was overreacting to him, that this was just kind of a throwback high school crush. I'd been having similar reactions lately to actors being interviewed on Bravo. But the truth was I couldn't even remember how long it had been since I'd had any one-on-one contact with an attractive, heterosexual, attentive man my age. Make that any age.

Jeff didn't really count. We'd been together so long that I had to remind myself to look at him. Usually it would take a comment from one of my friends, or even a glance from another woman as we were sitting in a restaurant, for me to notice again that my husband is good-looking. It was that way with my house, too. Someone would walk in and say, "Wow, great house," and I'd look around and see it with fresh eyes.

David had his arms crossed over his chest and he was looking at me and still smiling. "Earth to March," he said.

"Sorry," I said. I was developing a serious apology habit, I noticed. I'd worked on that kind of thing several times with clients. "I'd just like to know a little bit more about why you want to do this show."

David uncrossed his arms. "Okay, here's the deal. I think it could make some money. I also think it might be a good show and, as the only two potentially sane adults on the premises, it would be fun to work together. But, don't get me wrong. Money is the big motivator. I've been watching and waiting since I got here about a year ago, and this is the first thing that's looked like an opportunity."

"So we're talking broker time here? Selling ads, syndicating it ourselves, the whole bit?" I loved this stuff. I felt a surge of the same excitement I'd felt when I started my directionality business. And my party planning and aerobics businesses.

David was nodding. "You might as well hear the whole story. A little over a year ago, I was the victim of a bank merger. Sixteen years of an excruciatingly boring career as a loan officer, then a manager—over just like that. Actually, first they had me train my replacement, and then they pushed me out the door."

"I'm so sorry."

"Not as sorry as my wife is. She's got a good job, but we're dipping into our college fund, and we have two daughters who are going to need it in a couple of years." He reached one hand to the back of his neck and gave it a quick massage. "But my whole life people have been telling me I have a radio voice and I just had to give it a shot. You know? So I'm on the air, two hours at A.M. drive time, and I love it, but I'm not making enough money to justify my transgression."

I made a mental note to tune in to him tomorrow morning, sort of like scheduling some fantasy time. "So, how long a grace period did Dickerman give us before we have to pay for air time?"

"Ninety days."

"Wow, you're good."

"Why, thank you." David blew on his closed fist, polished his fingernails on his chest, then smiled again. "Okay, so here's the question: How much of this show do you want in on?"

"All of it."

●

Today *Karyn's Karmic Korner* was going to lead right into *I'm Rubber, You're Glue*. Olivia and I would sit in on Karyn's show and plug ours a few times in the hopes that Karyn's audience might stick around for us. Then Karyn was going to stay with us during our show until we got the hang of things and, as soon as she was gone, we'd move into her time slot.

"How're you doing, honey?" I asked Olivia while we sat at the long, narrow wood-grained table waiting for Karyn to show up for her show.

Olivia didn't even seem to be annoyed with me for anything. She scrunched her shoulders up to her ears. "Isn't this so exciting? I've been telling everybody. Did you remember to tell Dad and Jackson to listen?"

"Of course." Karyn fluttered into the room wearing yards and yards of something green and gauzy. I gave her a big smile and said, "Thanks so much for helping us get our new show off the ground."

"Don't worry, they're actually paying me for a half hour. Okay, listen. I've only got a minute for you two because I have to get my head in the right space for my show. But, okay, which one of you is Rubber and which one is Glue so I can make the intro flow?"

"Oh, she's Glue, all right," Olivia said, but at least she smiled when she said it.

"No way," I said. "I am so totally Rubber you're not going to believe it."

Karyn reached through the sea of fabric to find her chair and pull it closer to the table. "I don't know," she said. "I think the energy's all wrong if you use manmade materials. Although possibly rubber counts as natural. I think you should make it *I'm Fire, You're Water* or even *I'm Earth, You're Air*."

"I think we should stay away from your territory," I said.

"That's a good point," Karyn said. "The void I leave when I move on should remain until it makes sense cosmically for it to be filled."

"Ten seconds," David's voice said.

Karyn closed her eyes, and when she opened them her voice was lower. "Greetings. This is *Karyn's Karmic Korner* and today we're going to discuss how your wardrobe personality is directly tied to your sun sign. Take me, I'm an Aquarian, so everything I wear has to be completely cutting edge."

●

Olivia and I kept waiting for Karyn to say something about our show.

"You won't forget about our show, will you?" I said every time we took a break. Karyn would shake her head, then slump forward on the table while she waited for the commercial to be over.

"Plug the show," David even said before he said, "ten seconds." Then he wrote it on the whiteboard in big letters and held it up for Karyn to see.

"And that's it for today's *Karyn's Karmic Korner*. Just remember Karma. Is. A boomerang. Oh, wait. I almost forgot. We have another show starting today right after . . ."

That was all anybody listening got to hear, since the show's final music, which today consisted of waterfalls and wooden flutes, came in loud and strong at that point. Karyn stopped talking and shrugged her bony shoulders. "Sorry, I just got so into it that I forgot all about you."

"I think my wardrobe personality is much hotter than my sun sign," Olivia said. "Can that happen?"

"Yeah, probably. There are all sorts of factors, like how close you were to any cusps when you were born. Listen, I think we should talk about your show. Has anybody showed you how to work the call-in lines?"

Olivia and I both shook our heads.

"Well, if one of them lights up, then there's somebody on it. That's about it."

The door opened and Justin and Caitlin carried two kitchen chairs into the room. "We thought you might need some faces," Caitlin said.

"Dude. I just finished your theme-song tape. It totally rocks."

"We have a theme song?" Olivia said. "Will I like it?"

"Shh," Karyn said. "So, how do you want me to introduce you?"

"Ten seconds," the voice said.

"Don't worry," I told Karyn. "I'll take care of it."

The theme song came on and I recognized it immediately as the "Red Rubber Ball" of my childhood. It was the first 45 I'd ever owned. Maybe Justin's mother and I could switch children. I almost forgot what I was going to say but, as the music faded out, I glanced down at my notes and pulled myself back together.

"Good afternoon. This is March Monroe and I'm here with

my daughter, Olivia, to host a brand-new show here at WQBM called *I'm Rubber, You're Glue*. It's a great pleasure for both of us to be here, but I can tell you that's about the only thing we're ever going to agree on during this or any other show. So call in right this minute and bounce your ideas and questions off us and see how they stick. And, now, a word from our local sponsors . . ."

I was pretty proud of myself, especially my bounce and stick line, so I was surprised to see the whiteboard appear in the window. *No sponsors,* it said. I knew that.

"Okay," I said. "Apparently we're so brand-new we don't quite have any sponsors yet. So how about picking up your phone and calling in now. The number is, um . . ." I squinted at the front of the phone. "781-555-5000."

I raised my eyebrows in the direction of my daughter the cohost, hoping for a little support. "That's 781-555-5000," she said in a shaky voice.

All five of us looked at the phone. I thought I saw a light starting to come on, but it must have been my imagination. Justin waved his hands back and forth, then pointed to himself.

"I think we have a phone call," I said. I looked at Justin. "Hello, you're on the air."

Justin held a fist beside his jaw, extending his thumb up toward his ear and his pinkie in the opposite direction. He spoke into his pinkie. "Quite right. Quite right," he said into his imaginary phone in his phony English accent. "I'd like to comment on the bloody good theme music that was just now giving a play on my roadster radio. Bloody marvelous choice, that."

"And what's your first name, caller?" I asked.

"Lord Devonshire the Third." Justin adjusted some imaginary lapels even though he was actually wearing an *I Love Lucy* T-shirt.

"Well," I said, ignoring the name. "I'd have to say I think the theme music is great, too. 'Red Rubber Ball' was the first forty-five I ever owned. Now what was the name of the band that played it again . . ."

Justin leaned into Olivia's microphone. "The Cyrkle. 1966. Lyrics by Paul Simon and Bruce Woodley." His accent seemed to have disappeared, I noticed.

"Cyrkle," I said. "That name doesn't even sound familiar. And are you sure Paul Simon cowrote it?"

"Dude, absolutely. Another little-known fact is that the Cyrkle was the opening act on the Beatles' final U.S. tour. And 'Turn Down Day' was another big hit of theirs. Great sitar music on that one."

Karyn perked up. " 'Red Rubber Ball,' " she said. "That would be a fire element. Oh, by the way, it's me, Karyn from *Karyn's Karmic Korner*. You might say I'm here to bring good karma to a brand-new show."

I knew I had to move things in the direction the show was supposed to be going. I'd never really had to try to push Olivia's buttons before; it just came naturally. "I'm sure my daughter, Olivia, remembers that song," I said. "I used to play it when she and her brother were little and the whole family would dance around the house. Don't you remember how much you loved that song, Olivia?"

I pointed to the microphone. "No," she said in a tiny voice.

"You were so cute," I added. "I think that was the same year we took that really sweet picture of you in the bathtub. Naked."

Olivia looked at me wordlessly.

One of the buttons on the phone lit up, and we all looked at it as if we'd seen a miracle. Karyn reached over, pushed the button, and lifted the receiver off the hook and handed it to me. She nodded.

"Hello, this is *I'm Rubber, You're Glue*. We're live on WQBM Radio and you're on the air," I said. "What's your first name, caller?"

"This isn't Sylvia's Country Florists?"

"No," I admitted. "But what were you going to ask her?"

•

As soon as the show was over, David's voice came over the microphone. "March," he said, "can you come in here for a minute?"

I walked from the conference room into the hallway, then opened the adjacent door to let myself into the studio. I shut the door to the studio behind me, and David flipped a switch near his microphone. "What happened to your daughter?" he asked.

"I don't know. She's never been that passive—not even when I was pregnant with her."

David drummed his fingers on the counter in front of him. "Don't worry. We have some time. And I think I have a couple of ideas."

"Well, I'm glad one of us does. I'm still not so sure this show is a good idea."

He widened his eyes and stuck out his lower lip. "Okay. Well, I suppose I can always find another bank job. Or rob one."

I smiled. "That's too much guilt for me. You must have been

a great teenager. All right, I'll hang in there for a while." I gave him a little wave and turned and pushed open the door. Olivia was waiting in the hallway. "What were you doing in there?" she asked.

"Talking to David about ways we can improve our show."

"So it's David now."

"Olivia, what's that supposed to mean?"

"It's my show, too. Why wasn't I in there with you?" Olivia rubbed her palm up and down her cheek, the way she always did when she was trying not to cry. "I ruined the whole show, didn't I?"

"Oh, honey." I took a risk and hugged her. She stayed fairly stiff but didn't try to pull away. I stroked her hair and smelled the strawberry scent of her conditioner. "You're just not used to being on the air. You'll be better before you know it."

Olivia stiff-armed me away from her. "So, what, you thought I was that bad? Maybe if you weren't always hogging all the attention, I might have had a chance to say something."

For a split second I wanted to kill her. I summoned up a picture of her as an infant, wrapped in her soft pink blankie, helpless and sweet. Completely nonverbal. "Oh, sweetie," I said, "I think you're wonderful. Everything will be just fine."

"You know, Mom, you're really starting to get mood swings. You're not exactly the easiest person to be around lately. Do you think I could have twenty dollars?"

"You're out of money already?"

"Mom, do you have any idea how much toilet paper costs?"

"No, Olivia. I've never had to buy any."

"See what I mean? There was no reason to talk to me like that."

"Just tell me how your father and I can be paying almost

forty thousand dollars a year to BU without the toilet paper being included?"

Olivia shook her head. "Okay, maybe toilet paper was a bad example. But you can't always count on there being any left on the weekends, and I'm getting really sick of the food in the cafeteria. And, I don't know, I just didn't think an extra twenty was too much to ask for. But, never mind, I don't even want it now."

"Okay, well, I'm going to take off now so I don't hit traffic."

"Yeah, well, thanks a lot, Mom."

15

You cannot change what

○ a. you do not acknowledge
○ b. you don't really want to change
○ c. is a product of your genes
○ d. you look like in jeans

"We thought we'd surprise you with dinner," Jeff said as I walked into the kitchen. "It was so nice out there, we decided to pretend it was still summer and have a cookout."

I checked out the hotdogs and hamburgers, Boston baked beans and Cape Cod potato chip scattered across the counter. Not just dinner, but premeditated dinner. Jeff must have stopped after work. "Why were you surprising me?" I asked. "Did you forget to listen to the show?"

Jackson must have gone, too, judging by the plastic container of green ketchup he was opening. "Wow, she's unbelievable, Dad. You can't get away with anything."

"Thanks, kiddo. Sorry, honey, I was in a meeting. I just couldn't do it. You can get a tape from the station, can't you? We'll all listen to it together." He grabbed a plate of hamburgers that he'd pressed into perfectly executed patties. "Be right back," he said.

"Fine," I said.

"So, how'd it go?" Jackson asked. He squirted green ketchup into the opening of a hotdog roll and started to eat it. I tried not to look.

"You missed it, too?" I opened the refrigerator and pulled out a bottle of seltzer.

"Sorry, Mom, I lost track of time. Did you and Olivia scratch each other's eyes out?"

"Jackson. You know it's not supposed to be like that. At least not exactly like that. And as it turned out, Olivia hardly said a word the whole time."

"Maybe it only works when you don't want her to say anything."

Jeff walked back in and grabbed the hotdogs. "I think we should breed her," he said.

"Olivia?" I asked.

Jackson made a choking sound. I watched to make sure he was breathing. "Mom, don't do that when I'm eating. Like you could find someone to breed with Olivia." He squirted some ketchup onto the end of his finger.

"Flighty," Jeff said. "I think we should breed Flighty. It's one of the best cures for excessive egg laying."

I took a long sip of my seltzer, thinking as soon as I was hydrated, I might have to switch to wine. "She's laid exactly two eggs, Jeff. That's hardly excessive."

"Dad, she only laid the second one because you took the first one away from her. I told you she'd be traumatized."

"So, Jeff, I was just telling Jackson that Olivia hardly said a word during our show."

"Did you know," Jackson said, "that calico cats, which are black and white, and tortoiseshells, which are black and orange, are almost always female?"

"You don't say," Jeff said. He turned around and walked back outside.

Jackson's green finger disappeared briefly into his mouth. I moved the bottle of ketchup away. "Yeah," he said. "It's because every female cat receives one X chromosome from her mother and one X chromosome from her father, while a male receives one X chromosome from his mother and one Y chromosome from his father. The gene for coat color is in the X chromosome. So, if one of the X's is black and the other X is white or orange, then you'd get a calico or a tortoiseshell. Isn't that cool?"

"Fascinating," I said, even though I'd lost him about halfway. "As long as it's not encouraging you to become sexually active."

"Mom, that's disgusting." Jackson poured himself a glass of milk.

"Sorry. I thought you liked it when I made jokes."

"Only if they're funny."

"It was funny when it was about Olivia."

"What's your point?"

Jeff came back in for the rolls. I'd never understood the way he did one thing at a time. Multitasking was so much more efficient. I would have brought everything out at the same time, and pulled some weeds while I waited. "I've been reading up on it," he said. "I measured and Flighty's cage is big enough for two. So all we have to do is hang a nest box in the cage. Actually, the book said you hang it on the outside of the cage, though I don't quite get how the birds get to it if it's outside the cage. Maybe it was a typo. I'll have to ask the vet. But, anyway, the incubation period is twenty-one days."

"I've been wondering," Jackson said. "Do you guys think I can get a ferret?"

"Sure, honey," I said. "As soon as you get your first apartment, Dad and I will buy you one as a housewarming gift."

"Why do I get the feeling no one is listening to me?" Jeff asked.

"Actually, I was trying to tell you about Olivia's and my show. The one you missed . . ."

Jackson sniffed the air. "Does anybody else smell something burning?"

While Jeff ran out to rescue dinner, the phone rang. I took another sip of my seltzer, then walked over to the kitchen phone to check the number on the caller ID. When I saw that it was Olivia's cell phone number, I actually thought about not answering, or telling Jeff or Jackson to get it. I took a deep breath and picked up the phone.

"Hello," I said.

"Mom, it's me. My mouth hurts. A lot."

Probably from all those nasty things you were saying to me, I wanted to say. "Where?" I said instead, indulging myself with just a hint of my hurt mother's voice.

"Way in the back, where my wisdom teeth are."

Damn. It had been months since the dentist had given us

that referral slip to an oral surgeon. There'd been so much going on, and we were still paying Jackson's orthodontist bills. I just sort of figured she could slide by until next summer to have them taken out. "Well," I said. "It's probably your wisdom teeth then. Do you have Extra Strength Tylenol?"

"Yeah, but, Mom, you don't understand. Both sides hurt, but one side really, really hurts."

"Honey, what can I do now?" I squinted at the clock on the stove. "It's six-thirty. I'll call first thing in the morning and get you in to see the oral surgeon as soon as I can, okay? I'll call you as soon as I have an appointment."

"Okay. Mom?"

"Yeah?"

"Thanks."

•

When I arrived at Etta's house for my Quantum Physics and You tutoring session, she was cleaning out her garage. It had turned out that Etta lived in Rocky Point, a couple of miles from my house. So much for going to Olde Colony to meet a broader cross section of people—I could have just stayed home.

I parked on the street since three distinct piles of assorted stuff threatened to take over her entire driveway. Etta lived in the house I wanted but would probably never be able to afford. Even from here I could see that it had its very own stairway leading from the seawall down to the beach. It was one of those houses that would sell to a wealthy person in a minute, only to be torn down and replaced with a dream house. I loved it just the way it was, and was glad Etta could still afford to pay the taxes on it.

Etta was tall and had fairly broad shoulders, but she was absolutely swimming in an old zip-up sweatshirt that must have belonged to either her son or her late husband. The sleeves were rolled up so many times they looked like bracelets, and there was enough loose fabric in the hood she'd tied in a jaunty bow under her chin, that it puckered all around her head. Ringlets of white poked out from underneath and framed her face. "Why in God's name would I hang on to half a can of paint for twenty years when I never liked the color in the first place, can you answer me that, March?"

"Hi, Etta. Let's see now, what have we here." I considered each category then pointed to them in turn. "Save, Throw Away, and Can't Decide?"

"No, I'd have to say it's more Know I Should But Couldn't Bear To, Know I Should and Maybe I Will, and Get Rid of It."

"Well, at least you've got a system."

"Still, I haven't any use for a single scrap of it. I mean, really, March." She picked up a hose that looked like it might have once belonged to the world's first vacuum cleaner and swung it around her shoulders like a boa. "You know, you spend the first half of your life collecting everything you can get your hands on, then the second half trying to find someone to give it all away to. See anything you want?"

I smiled. "Thanks, but I'm not even going to look. You should see *my* garage. What about Edward?"

"Edward." Etta shook her head. "I saved all of it for Edward, and now he and his wife like to buy everything brand spanking new. Look at these." Etta pulled two miniature bamboo rakes from a stack of gardening equipment. "All these years later, they're in perfect condition. We had two of them so Edward and a friend could rake leaves into a pile to jump on."

She placed the two little rakes side by side on the crushed stone of the driveway, then pulled out a full-sized version of the same rake. She leaned her chin on the handle, looking like a white-haired Cinderella about to sweep the floor. "They'd rake away on their own for the first bit of time, then they'd come running into the house to find me, and Edward would say, 'Mummy, quick, get the big rake, we need more engine power.' "

"Olivia and Jackson always loved to rake leaves," I said. I'd jumped right in and started sorting through an old wooden tool box. I started making a line of identically sized flathead screwdrivers at the edge of the Get Rid of It pile. "At least until they hit adolescence and became allergic to any activity that might be helpful. Their favorite thing was to stuff the leaves into an old flannel shirt and jeans, then add a pumpkin head to make a scarecrow."

I stood back for a moment and counted the duplicate screwdrivers: nine. "Olivia lost interest after a while, but Jackson kept up the tradition. And then a couple of years later I came home one day, and the scarecrow was hanging from a tree, headless, with a noose around its neck, and I knew my sweet little boy was a teenager."

"It all goes by too fast, doesn't it?" Etta blew her nose with a piece of tissue she'd tucked up under one rolled sleeve. "Well, enough. You didn't come here to help me clean. Let's get you up to snuff before the next exam."

I tried to imagine facing a huge clean-up project like this without Jeff. I couldn't. "Why not? I'd do just about anything to avoid quantum physics for a few more minutes."

"You, my dear March, are an angel."

"Okay, let's get to work." I walked into the garage, stood on my tiptoes, pulled an old wooden sled off a hook, and walked it out to Know I Should But Couldn't Bear To pile. "Have you given any more thought to Edward's Elder Hostel suggestion? I still think New Zealand is a great idea."

Etta placed a miniature wooden rocker next to the sled. When she looked up she was grinning. "I must admit I sent him a counter-suggestion. A newspaper article about a Caribbean charter, the first clothing-optional flight on a commercial airline. History in the making, and I told Edward I think I'd very much like to be a part of it."

I tried to picture it. "Wouldn't you worry about who'd been sitting on the seat before you?"

"It's quite well thought out. They pass around towels to sit on. And they heat up the cabin until it's nice and toasty. Eventually, when you reach a certain altitude, the pilot wishes you a lovely flight and tells you it's safe to unbuckle and disrobe, and to move about the cabin freely."

I laughed. "Would you really do it? I wouldn't have the guts. Not even back when I still sort of liked my body."

"I don't know. I suppose I was only trying to get Edward's goat by sending him something racy. That boy won't be happy until I've started crocheting doilies."

I would have loved to have a mother like Etta, to open up one of her letters from Florida to find a racy article instead of gossip from her condo complex and complaints about my father. Edward had no idea how lucky he was.

I picked up one of the small rakes we'd looked at earlier. "If you don't mind," I said, "I think I might take you up on these rakes. I have an idea for them."

My cell phone rang just as we'd finally cracked open our Quantum Physics and You books. Actually it played a few bars from "Wild Thing," something Jackson had programmed for me and I'd never figured out how to change. It became embarrassingly louder as I hunted through my bag for it.

"Hello," I said finally.

"Hi, it's me," Jeff said. "We're just leaving the oral surgeon's office now."

I mouthed *sorry* to Etta. "So, how did it go?" I asked Jeff.

"Well, he pointed out that the referral slip is over six months old, but after I apologized for you . . ."

"For me? What did I have to do with it?" Etta looked up with interest. I lowered my voice and adjusted my tone until I was speaking calmly. "You know how to make appointments. Olivia knows how to make appointments. I had a million other things to do. Why am I the heavy here?"

"Okay, I apologized for all of us. Anyway, after that and after he saw how much pain Olivia was in, he said they'd squeeze her in this week. The day after tomorrow. Twelve-thirty. Nothing to eat or drink from midnight tomorrow night. A responsible adult needs to be with her to drive her home afterward. Sixteen hundred dollars and our insurance doesn't cover it. Listen, I've got to go. Olivia has a class and I have to get back to work."

I was still not happy about the apology comment, but I let it go and said good-bye pleasantly. "It's always something," I said to Etta as soon as I hung up. "My daughter has to have her wisdom teeth out the day after tomorrow."

"Well, good luck, dear," Etta said. "She's going to be quite miserable for a spell. I know Edward was."

I guess I could have asked for details, but I figured I'd find out soon enough. Besides, even I knew it was past time to get to work on quantum physics. I didn't have another minute to waste.

16

When your children have all finally left home

- ○ a. your husband will still be there
- ○ b. you'll have a really big party
- ○ c. you'll miss them more than you expected
- ○ d. they'll come back just to drive you crazy

"Well, I can't take her," Jeff said. "I'll be playing catch up all week after taking off so much time today."

"Oh, all right," I said. "I was hoping to spend some time at the station on Friday, although I guess it can wait till next week. But she should come home with you tomorrow night after work and spend the night here. Then I won't have to drive in and pick her up on Friday morning."

Jeff finished slicing a tomato and dumped it into the center of the salad with no thought to presentation. "We already worked that part out. She said she'll come home with me tomorrow night and do her laundry, then stay up late and write a paper she has due, and wake up just before the surgery so she won't get too hungry."

I wondered if I could ever sleep until noon no matter how late I'd gone to bed, even though I'd done it quite well all through my twenties. Now some nights I found myself nodding off about eight-thirty. I decorated the top of the salad with a ring of broccoli florets, then handed it to Jeff. At least I'd have a little chunk of time on Friday morning before Olivia woke up. Maybe I'd take a walk by myself. Maybe I'd catch up on a few things. Maybe I'd wait and see how I felt.

I carried the veggie lasagna into the dining room. "Smells good," Jeff said, pulling out his chair. "I'm starving."

"Me, too," Jackson yelled from the kitchen. He'd just poured seltzer for me and filtered water for Jeff, and had gone back to get something for himself. He returned carrying three glasses of milk. I raised my eyebrows. "What?" he said. "You're the one who made the rule about no milk cartons on the table."

"He's got you there," Jeff said.

Jackson took a long drink from one of his glasses, then wiped his mouth. "Mom, Feral's still scratching at her ears and shaking her head. Can we take her to the vet tomorrow?"

"Oh, all right," I said. "I'll see if I can get an appointment."

"You know," Jeff said, "Flighty's still acting strange, too, and I keep finding feathers on the bottom of the cage. Maybe you can take her, too."

●

I made a mad dash to the grocery store, filling my cart with salad makings and several dinner options: a bag of frozen shrimp, a lean piece of steak, some boneless chicken. Then I added an assortment of après surgery snacks. Ben & Jerry's

Phish Food ice cream, Fudgsicles, Popsicles, lemon sorbet. Then vanilla yogurt, frozen strawberries, and ripe bananas to make smoothies. I was going for variety, since Olivia's eating habits seesawed as widely and as often as her moods. One day she'd be eating healthy, the next day she'd be counting calories, and the next day she'd just be eating or not eating. At least I knew I could count on Jeff and Jackson to polish off everything she turned up her nose at.

I swung by my house to put the groceries away quickly. Feral rubbed against my ankle and meowed. I gave her a chicken-flavored Pounce, and she batted it across the kitchen and toward the family room, where I knew she'd have to stalk and kill the heavily processed morsel of food before she ate it. "Don't get lost," I warned. "You have an appointment this afternoon."

I checked the kitchen clock, then settled for a quick banana and bowl of yogurt for lunch. I scooped out a single spoonful of Phish Food. While I was eating it, I put the container back in the refrigerator before I got greedy. I grabbed my car keys again and headed for Ahndrayuh's house.

Clark was sitting on the front steps when I pulled into the driveway. He ran over to the car and opened my door. "Hi," I said. "What are you doing home from school? Don't you dare breathe on me if you're sick."

He laughed like I was kidding. "I'm not sick, silly," he said. I made sure his hand was out of the way before I closed the car door. "It's an early release day. That means the teachers get out early to learn how to teach better. It makes my mother crazy."

"Well, it's a good thing they did it today, because I brought you all presents." I opened the door to the backseat and leaned inside.

Clark pushed in beside me. "Wow."

I straightened up and handed Clark one of the three bamboo rakes I'd pulled out. "Here you go," I said.

"Thanks," he said.

"You're welcome," I said.

He held the handle of the rake in one hand and used the other to push his glasses closer to his face. "I've seen these," he said. "What do you do with them again?"

"Clark," I said. "Haven't you ever used a rake before?" He shook his head back and forth. "How do you get rid of the leaves when they fall off your trees?"

"Men in a truck suck them up with a big hose," he said.

By the time Ahndrayuh and Hillary found us, we had a pretty good pile going. "Look, Mom," Clark said. "March is teaching me how to rake leaves into a pile. And after we're done, I get to jump in them."

"Me, too," Hillary said, reaching for the other small rake.

"Fun," Ahndrayuh said. "I'll be right back. I think I hear the phone."

I fumed for a couple of minutes while I raked. I mean, what was I, the baby-sitter? Though, come to think of it, it was pretty good money for baby-sitting and, according to my calculations, we had only one session left. "I'll be right back," I said to Clark and Hillary. "I need to talk to your mother."

Fortunately, Ahndrayuh had left the back door open. She was in the kitchen, sitting on a stool at her granite counter and flipping through a copy of *Self* magazine. "Excuse me," I said, "but I'm here to work with you."

Ahndrayuh looked up and refocused her turquoise eyes on me. "Have you ever noticed how hard it is for people to leave you if they can't find you to tell you?"

"Huh?" I said. Just the thought of trying to follow that one gave me a headache.

"I just don't want you to quit, that's all."

I decided to take a stab at brutal honesty. "But we don't really even like each other."

"That's not the point. I have a hard time letting go of things even if I don't like them."

I closed my eyes for a minute. I'd spent so many years doing things I didn't really want to do for people I didn't really like. Driving carpool when it wasn't really my turn because I just wanted to avoid the confrontation. Hanging on to friendships that had long passed their expiration dates. I'd spent a whole year dodging one of Jackson's friend's mothers who wanted to be my new best friend even though we had absolutely nothing in common. She was always dropping by with pesto she'd just made or a book she thought I'd enjoy. I felt so guilty about not reciprocating that I once even stopped by when I knew she wouldn't be home and left a note that said, *Sorry I missed you.*

"Ahndrayuh," I said firmly. "The next session will be our last. Please spend some time thinking about how you'd like to use it."

"Second to last." Ahndrayuh lifted up her magazine until it hid her face. "I still need time to adjust and you don't want me to be traumatized. You wouldn't be able to live with yourself."

●

Jackson must have heard the car because he opened the kitchen door for me. "Hi, honey," I said. "Grab a quick snack if you haven't eaten, and then we have to take Feral to the vet."

Jackson reached into the freezer and pulled out the Phish Food. "I thought we were taking Flighty, too." He took out a cereal bowl and started shoveling ice cream into it.

"Sweetie, don't eat all of that, okay? Have a banana or something." I drank a glass of water to distract me from the pull of the Phish Food. "I don't think Flighty's cage will even fit in the van. Remember, we had to take it apart to get it home."

"I'll hold on to her."

"A cat and a bird in the car at the same time. Now why don't I think that's a good idea."

"They're friends, Mom."

"Jackson, trust me on this one. We'll take Feral today. Dad made up a list of questions to ask the vet about Flighty. If they think we should bring her in, we'll make another appointment."

Jackson went off to lure Feral into the travel cage we'd originally bought to capture her in. As with Flighty, we'd never planned on having a cat. She'd started coming around the house in the late summer about three years ago—no, it was four now. She was a stray, not much more than a kitten, thin and scraggly with the most pitiful meow I'd ever heard.

Despite the name Jackson insisted on, she was more of a panhandler than a true feral cat. She'd show up in our yard every couple of days, hang around giving us hungry looks until someone broke down and fed her, and then disappear. It always felt to me that she'd auditioned the entire neighborhood for the part of family, and somehow chose ours. I was ridiculously flattered by her validation of us, even though we'd probably just been more generous with table scraps than anyone else.

In my heart I'd given in to her long before I admitted it.

Eventually she started coming close enough to pat, and Jeff called the vet to ask what we should do. The vet suggested we capture her and bring her to the animal shelter so she could be given her shots, spayed, and, with luck, adopted. We could try enticing her into a carrier cage first, and if that didn't work we could borrow a trap from the shelter. So we bought a cheap blue plastic carrying cage with a little white handle, put a frayed bathroom towel on the bottom, and some pieces of string cheese on top of that.

We left it on the front porch and she walked right in. And of course we kept her.

•

"How long has she been scratching her ears like that?" the vet asked. A wave of guilt washed over me. I wondered how harmful it would be for Jackson to hear me shave a few weeks off the truth.

"Forever," Jackson said before I had time to answer.

The vet pursed his lips together, and put the scope into Feral's other ear. He made soft, soothing sounds while Feral struggled to get away from the assistant who held her tucked under an arm. Finally, the vet looked up at me. I felt like I did when my dental hygienist raised an eyebrow and asked, *How often did you say you've been flossing?*

"We can give her medicine to get rid of the ear mites, but these ears are seriously inflamed. I think we should put her in an Elizabethan collar to keep her from scratching and give them some time to heal."

I'd pictured something in jeweled velvet, but the collar turned out to be a white plastic inverted lampshade. Feral liked it even less than I did. She paced the floor of the small examining room, scratching at it instead of her ears, while I asked the vet about Flighty.

I took out Jeff's list and skipped over all the breeding questions. I certainly wasn't going to be an enabler when it came to that particular hobby. "We keep finding feathers on the bottom of the cage," I said. "Should we have her looked at?" I hoped the use of the word *we* instead of *my husband* would redeem me somewhat in the vet's eyes. This, too, was very much like my irrational need to be liked by my dental hygienist. What was wrong with me that I couldn't just say, *Sorry, I haven't had a minute to think about my cat's ears* or *I understand it's important in your life but, you know, I'm just not that into flossing.*

"If it continues, bring her in and we'll run some diagnostic tests," the vet was saying. "Birds use their feathers for a variety of things. Obviously, to fly. But also to regulate their temperature, to protect themselves from the environment, and to attract the opposite sex."

"I think she's trying to find a bird to fertilize her egg," Jackson said.

"Are there other birds in the household?"

"No," I said quickly.

"Well, then. Let's see, feather picking rarely happens with cockatiels, but that's the biggest thing you want to look out for. Just don't start giving her any attention for it. Birds are a lot like children, and negative attention can often seem better than no attention at all."

17

I am happiest when I am

○ a. with my friends and family
○ b. learning something new
○ c. eating chocolate
○ d. asleep

Olivia and Jeff were laughing as they walked into the house. As soon as she saw me, Olivia stopped. "My mouth is killing me," she said, covering one side of her face with her palm.

Jeff gave Olivia a sympathetic look, one of many, I imagined, since they'd left Boston for Rocky Point. He gave me a kiss as he walked past me, then punched Jackson playfully on the shoulder and headed upstairs. He liked to change out of his work clothes as soon as he got home.

"Hey, Dad," Jackson yelled after him. "Wait till you see Feral." Jackson turned back to Olivia. "Bet you'll look like a chipmunk by this time tomorrow."

Olivia put her other hand on her other cheek. "Thanks. I

missed you, too. You're even funnier looking than I remember you, Dorkface."

"I know you are, but what am I?"

"Come on you two, be nice," I said. "At least in front of me." I put Feral's tube of ointment on the windowsill over the kitchen sink so I wouldn't forget about it.

"We are being nice," Olivia said. "This is how we show our love, in case you haven't noticed." She stood on her tiptoes and kissed Jackson on the cheek.

"Ick. Disgusting." Jackson walked over to the sink, turned both faucets on full blast, and started splashing water on his face.

I picked an envelope up off the counter and handed it to Olivia. "From Gram," I said.

"Wow, that was quick." My mother was the kind of woman Hallmark kept inventing holidays for. Rarely an occasion went by that didn't warrant a card. Olivia opened this one, scanned quickly. She pulled out a charge card–shaped piece of plastic. "Great," she said. "Books R Us. Like I read."

"Well," Jackson said. "Maybe you can use it to buy yourself an ABC book and teach yourself. Or you could try to find a book that's just A and work your way up from there."

Olivia was busy giving her brother a nasty look, so I decided to hold off on reminding her to write a thank-you note to her grandmother. I opened the refrigerator to provide some distraction. "Okay, Olivia, since this is the last supper, it's your choice. I can do shrimp scampi, steak and baked potatoes, or chicken piccata."

"Make whatever you guys want. I'm not hungry. I think I'll just go up to my old room and chill. Then I have a paper to write."

Later that night I took a plate of the chicken piccata the rest of us had decided on up to Olvia's room. "Hey," she said when I knocked.

"Does that mean I can come in?" I asked.

"Yes, Mom, that means you can come in," she said as if I'd been joking. She was sitting cross-legged on her bed typing on her laptop.

"How's the paper coming?" I asked, putting the plate on her bedside table.

"Thanks," she said. She moved the laptop over and grabbed the plate. "Fine, I'm almost done with it."

"What class is it for?"

"Astronomy."

I sighed. "That's probably what I should have taken."

Olivia looked up from her plate. "Ohmigod, I never even thought to ask you what classes you were taking." She patted a spot next to her on the bed. It didn't seem to be a trap, so I sat down. "You know, you can always ask me if you need help or anything."

"Thanks, honey. You don't happen to know anything about quantum physics, do you?"

Olivia handed me the half-empty plate and shook her head. "Mom, what were you thinking? There are two choices for that requirement: Astronomy for Nonmajors and Rocks for Jocks. Period."

The door was open, but Jeff knocked anyway. "Can I come in?"

"Dad, did you know Mom is taking quantum physics?"

I let Jeff help only because he and Olivia ganged up on me. And I tried to pay attention while he made charts and took notes from my textbook in his precise block lettering, then read them aloud to me and told me what to think about them. Some of it even made a little bit of sense as he was saying it, but the truth was that as much as I knew I should appreciate his help, nothing had changed. He really got on my nerves whenever he tried to teach me anything.

We were sitting at the kitchen table, and I got up to make some tea. Not black tea to stay awake but herbal tea to sedate myself a little. He was so engrossed in what he was doing that he didn't seem to notice, and I wondered if I could get away with tiptoeing up to bed.

"Okay, March. Listen to this. All you have to do is think of . . ."

I sat back down again. "Jeff, do you remember that time we tried to wallpaper the bathroom together, and you were so focused on making sure we had plumb lines?"

Jeff took off his glasses and rubbed his eyes. "Huh?"

"And I thought that because it was an old house nothing was going to be plumb anyway, so it just had to look and feel right."

"Honey, it's late. I think you should stay on task here."

It wasn't that I didn't appreciate the notes. They might even come in handy once I could take a look at them alone. "Honey," I said just before I went up to bed. "You can tell me it's late, but you can't tell me what to do about it."

●

Jeff and I smoothed things over at breakfast. I thanked him for the great notes, even though I hadn't looked at them yet, and he said any time, and we both knew we wouldn't go there again for a while. After Jeff and Jackson went off to work and school, it felt very odd to have nowhere to be until 12:30. If I had dared, I would have peeked into Olivia's room just to remind myself what she looked like asleep in her own bed. Instead, I unloaded the dishwasher and threw a load of laundry into the washing machine.

I spent about a half hour with Jeff's notes, which were actually very helpful and much easier to take now that he was gone. After that, I couldn't decide whether I wanted to go out for a walk or to sit and enjoy the quiet. Feral wandered into the kitchen, shaking her head testily. The gray-and-white fur around her ears stuck together in little greasy clumps from the medicine. Olivia had oohed and aahed over Feral, and Jeff had let her sleep in his lap for a while, but Feral was still one unhappy cat in her plastic lampshade. She wedged herself in between my feet and crashed her head into one of my calves and then the other.

I decided to go out. I brought my cell phone with me, and left a note for Olivia, just in case she woke up and wondered where I was. It felt strange to be actually taking a walk without a client in tow. I found myself going through the list of everyone I knew in my mind to see if there was someone I should call.

My cell phone rang, and my first thought was that someone had somehow heard my thoughts and was calling me. It was Jeff. "Hi," he said. "I tried you at home but nobody answered. I'm on my way to a meeting with a client, and I was a few minutes early so I stopped at the grocery store. Do you remember what kind of baby food Olivia liked so much? Was it strained peaches? Or was it apricots?"

"Mixed fruit," I said. "But it had to be Junior Gerber. Why?"

"That's it. Okay, got it." I could hear what sounded like jars rolling around a shopping cart. One of our cell phones crackled with static then cleared. "I was just thinking that it might taste good to her after the surgery. I'd pick up some ice cream, too, but I'm afraid it would melt before I got home."

"Good call," I said. "We have plenty of ice cream anyway. Popsicles and Fudgsicles, too." I'd covered one block and half of another since the phone rang. My brain had become so wired for multitasking that it actually felt good to walk and talk at the same time. Maybe I'd have to develop a walkie-talkie workout for Ahndrayuh before I dumped her. Including her phone might be just the thing to finally get her motivated. I brought my attention back to Jeff. "But the baby food was a really sweet idea, Jeff. She loved that stuff. Remember, she was still asking for it when she was six?"

"I know, that's what made me think of it. Well, I'll be late for the meeting if I don't hurry. Good luck today."

"Thanks. You, too."

"Thanks. Love you."

"Love you, too," I said. There didn't seem to be any residual tension from our study session, which was a relief. I knew I'd overreacted, but I also knew I'd do it again the next time.

As soon as we hung up, I wondered if I should call some-one else, just to keep up my pace. It seemed like the first small step toward addiction, so I put my cell phone back in my jacket pocket. I started swinging both arms and lengthen-ing my stride a little. The bark on a birch tree I passed was amazingly white against the blue spruce behind it. The side-walk had a scattering of leaves, some colorful enough to war-rant being ironed between two sheets of wax paper. Olivia and Jackson used to love to do that. I probably still had some tucked into their baby books.

There's a time during almost every workout when it starts

to feel good, and I was well into it now. My body had lost its stiffness, my brain was soothed by the rhythm of my steps, and I felt like I could, maybe even should, walk forever. I was married to a man who might drive me crazy sometimes, but also one who would think to buy baby food for an eighteen-year-old. And I'd slept like a baby myself last night, with both kids at home and safely asleep in their beds. It just might not get any better than this.

●

I knocked on Olivia's bedroom door just before noon. "We have to leave in ten minutes, honey," I said.

"I know that," she said from the other side of the closed door. I walked back downstairs and waited. Sure enough, with a minute to spare, Olivia showed up in the kitchen. She was wearing loose flannel drawstring pants that looked like pajamas, and might well have been for all I could tell, with a loose-fitting short-sleeved T-shirt. "I can't believe I have to go out looking like this," she said.

She looked like she always looked to me, but I knew better than to say it. I pulled a printed sheet of paper out from under the magnet that had been holding it to the refrigerator. "Well, you've got to follow the instructions. I'm sure it's to make it easy for them to get the IV in." I handed it to Olivia. "Here. Just double-check to make sure you haven't missed anything."

Olivia glanced down at the sheet. "Shit," she said. "I forgot to take off my nail polish. Why the hell should I have to take off my nail polish?"

"I think it's so they can see your fingertips and your toes to check on your circulation."

"Why do they have to do that?"

"Honey, it's general anesthesia. They have to be careful."

Olivia looked up. She was always pale, but now she was very, very pale. "Mom, the surgeon showed me an X-ray of someone with eight wisdom teeth. I almost threw up."

I put my hand tentatively on her shoulder. "Honey, you only have four, I promise."

She didn't pull away. "And then he said he'd buy me a car if he broke my jaw."

"What kind of car?"

"Mom, I'm really scared." I slipped my hand behind her head and over to the other shoulder. She tucked her head into the crook of my neck, and I hugged her and breathed in the strawberry scent of her hair again.

"You'll be fine," I said, rocking her back and forth just a little bit. "It'll be over before you know it."

●

There were at least a dozen people in the waiting room so I had plenty of time to do the math. If half of them were designated drivers and the other half were patients, that meant six people each waiting to pay sixteen hundred dollars. One of my children would simply have to become an oral surgeon to support Jeff and me in our old age.

Certainly not the one seated beside me. Olivia was fanning herself with a magazine and looking whiter by the minute. "How much longer, do you think?" she whispered.

A woman seated across from us sighed loudly and said, "This." She sighed again and added, "is ridiculous."

I smiled at her noncommittally. I leaned over to Olivia and whispered, "Do you want to go get some fresh air? We can tell the receptionist we'll be right outside."

"No. I just want to get this over with."

A nurse opened the door to the waiting room and stood looking down at a clipboard. "Olivia Monroe?" she said. The woman across from us sighed again.

It was silly, but I felt an overwhelming sadness as I watched the nurse lead Olivia away. She looked so vulnerable. I tucked the little brown leather pocketbook she'd handed me into my black bag.

I'd brought the bag along just in case I was able to concentrate on working, but I couldn't. I picked up a magazine, put it back down, picked it up again. I tried fanning myself with it the way Olivia had. The cool air felt good in the stuffy waiting room. I closed my eyes.

18

You get what you

o a. give
o b. work for
o c. deserve
o d. marry

"Mrs. Monroe?" I'd been drifting somewhere between awake and asleep, and I jerked my head back, startled. The same nurse stood in the doorway with her clipboard. "You can go to the recovery room now." I checked my watch and saw that the whole thing had taken only thirty-three minutes. That was it, Jackson would have to be an oral surgeon whether he liked it or not. The quality of Jeff's and my golden years were at stake here. Either that or maybe Jeff could go back to school as soon as I finished.

The recovery room turned out to be a tiny postage stamp of a room, its single faux leather recliner and a small wooden chair taking up most of the space. The nurse peeked her head in first, then stood back to let me go inside. Olivia was sprawled across the upright recliner, gauze puffing her cheeks and poking out at the sides of her mouth. I sat down on the edge of the wooden chair and leaned toward her. She was staring up at the ceiling. "Hi, honey," I whispered.

Slowly her head swiveled toward me, her eyes still glassy from the anesthesia. "He called it a cocktail," she said through the gauze. "Ha ha ha." Her head switched directions and continued turning as if on ball bearings until she was looking over her shoulder. I felt a little bit like the mother in *The Exorcist* must have felt just before Linda Blair rotated her head a full 360 degrees.

Fortunately, my daughter's head stopped at about 180, at which point she said, "What kind of recliner is this? It doesn't recline." She flopped her head back against the headrest, which was touching the wall, and closed her eyes. *Ellen Burstyn*, I thought randomly, that's who played the mother in *The Exorcist*.

I considered my daughter draped before me, then turned to the nurse, who shrugged and said, "I'll be right back. You can get her up and moving any time."

I leaned in close and put my hand on Olivia's knee. "I think the chair is a little large for the room," I explained.

She opened her eyes. "Mommy!" Olivia pulled a wad of bloody gauze out of her mouth, looked at it for a moment, then put it back in. She looked at me again and smiled. "Hi, Mommy." She reached both hands up to me the way she used to almost twenty years ago when she wanted me to lift her out of her crib after a nap.

I held both of her hands and pulled her out of the nonreclining recliner, then bent down to pick up my bag. Olivia lurched by me and out to the hallway. "Watch me," she said. She held her arms out to her sides and placed one foot in front of the other as if she were trying to walk a straight line for a sobriety test. I didn't get an exact count, but somewhere around the third step, she teetered, took a quick toddle backward and pivoted sideways. She reached one hand out to hold on to the wall for support. I put my arm around her shoulder and she transferred her weight from the wall to me.

The nurse came back down the hallway. She glanced at Olivia, who'd closed her eyes again, then smiled at me. I didn't see anything the least bit funny. Seeing my daughter under the influence, even in these medically acceptable circumstances, was pushing my parental panic button. There was nothing rational about it, but I felt like I had opened the wrong door and walked in on my daughter in the midst of a wild college party. I wanted to lecture her. I wanted to ground her. Olivia lifted her head away from my shoulder, opened her eyes, and said, "Fuck."

The nurse handed me a prescription form. "Get one of these into her within the next hour." She handed me another. "And double up on the penicillin for the first dose. And buy two refillable ice packs and an Ace bandage to wrap around her head to hold them on." She handed me a list of instructions and I thought, *For sixteen hundred dollars, you can't throw in the ice packs?*

We made our way awkwardly through the overcrowded waiting room and out to the car. The fresh air seemed to revive Olivia, and she stood up all by herself while I opened the passenger door for her. I made sure her hands and feet were out of the way before I shut the door, then walked around to the driver's side.

As soon as I turned the key in the ignition, she started to laugh. "What?" I asked. I left the car in Park and turned to look at her.

Her eyes fought to stay focused on me. "Some responsible adult you are. You didn't even tell me to buckle." She laughed again, a muffled, gauzy sound, and tilted forward to turn on the radio.

After she managed to hit the button of a station that would drive me crazy all the way home, I reached over to buckle her seat belt for her. The last time I'd done this she'd been in a carseat. I knew it wasn't really fair, but I said it anyway. "Olivia, honey," I said, "I hope I never, ever see you like this again. Now let's get you home."

"Like what?" Olivia tried to rest her foot on the dashboard and missed, something she found inordinately funny. "I don't want to go home. I want to drive around. Come on, Mommy, let's drive around for a while."

I headed straight home, but I figured I might as well get a couple of questions in while she was in such a good, if drugged, mood. "So, honey," I asked, "how are things going with your roommate?"

"She sucks. But it's okay because both of us are never there." Olivia was playing with her window, pushing the button to roll it up and down in time with the music. "Next year I want a single in Sleeper Hall. Can you believe that's the real name?"

While Olivia laughed, I touched the lever to lock all four car doors. Just in case. I thought about what else I wanted to know, since I might never find her this responsive again. "So, Olivia, any cute boyfriends you've been meaning to tell me about?"

She left her window wide open and turned to look at me.

"Aww, Mom, that's an easy one . . ." The open window was blowing her hair into her face, and she stopped to pull a few strands out of her bloodstained, lopsided mouth. "Well, not really. But there's this guy in my dorm. His name is Rusty Wheelright. Try to say it, Mom, like really fast."

"Wusty Wheelwight," I said. "Oh, that poor boy."

"Well, you haven't seen him, Mom. He's pretty hot."

I reached over and brushed some hair out of her face. "He'd better be with a name like Wusty . . ."

"Ouch, my mouth hurts. Can we get some Popsicles?"

●

"Where is she?" I asked as soon as I got back from CVS. Jeff had offered to go to the store when I dropped Olivia off, but I'd thought it was only fair that he take a turn as caretaker.

Jeff was standing in front of the open refrigerator door, holding a jar of Gerber Mixed Fruit. "I think she's in singing to Flighty," he said. "I was just about to show her this."

Jackson walked into the kitchen. "Are we going to have anything for dinner tonight or are we just going to sit around and watch Olivia act like a drug addict?"

"What's she doing now?" I asked. I put the plastic CVS bag on the kitchen table and pulled out the ice packs.

Jackson shook his head. "She's trying to decorate Feral's lampshade with a marker. Let's just say it's not going over very well."

"I bet," I said. I threw the cardboard packaging away and held the ice packs out to Jeff. He put the baby food on the counter and took them. "Can you fill these up? I have to get this medicine into her. It's already been more than an hour." I handed the Ace bandage to Jackson. "Can you take this out of the box?"

Jackson examined the box. "I think I'll need a few more years of school before I can handle this much of a challenge, Mom."

"Cute," I said. I pulled the small pharmacy bag from the bottom of the larger plastic bag. I'd noticed that our prescription copayments had gone up again. After we finished paying for Olivia's wisdom teeth and anything else that hadn't been covered by our insurance, we'd be hitting our equity loan again just to pay the bills this month. I decided to give Jackson a little nudge in the right direction. "By the way, how would you feel about a lucrative career as an oral surgeon?"

"You should have asked him yesterday," Jeff said. "Then he could have taken out Olivia's wisdom teeth."

"Gee, sorry I missed it," Jackson said. He handed me the Ace bandage and dropped the shredded cardboard on the kitchen counter. I gave him a look and he started cleaning up his mess. "Actually, I was thinking if I got really good at gambling, you and Dad might send me to Vegas."

"That's my boy," Jeff said. An ice cube missed one of the bags and skittered across the tile floor.

Feral meowed loudly and walked into the room. Olivia followed. Her face was really starting to swell, more on one side than the other. "Why are there feathers all over the bottom of Flighty's cage?" she asked. "Can I have them?"

"Pretend you don't notice," Jeff said. "We're not supposed to call attention to them."

"Oops, too late." Olivia put her hand up to her mouth. "Ouch."

I put on my reading glasses and scanned the two prescription bottles. "Okay, one says take on an empty stomach, and the other says take with food. So, you're going to take two of these, eat a little something, then one of these. After that, we'll get this ice on you." I handed her two pills and a glass of water. She swallowed them down, and a small stream of water ran out one side of her mouth. She didn't appear to notice.

Jeff smiled. "Here you go, honey. Look what I got you." He twisted the top of the baby food jar and the seal broke with a pop. "Yum. Mixed fruit. Baby Girl's very favorite."

"Oh, Daddy, that is so adorable." Olivia managed to walk her way over to him in a fairly straight line. He handed her the jar and she squinted at the label. "Holy shit. Do you know how many calories are in this stuff? Don't we have anything else to eat around here?"

I opened both the refrigerator and the freezer doors as wide as they went so she could look for herself. Jeff and I exchanged looks. "Well," he said. "How about if I go out and pick up a couple of pizzas for the rest of us. You want to come, too, sport?"

"Oh, yeah," Jackson said.

Jeff was already halfway to the door. "We'll rent some videos, too. Anything special you want to see, Olivia?"

Olivia pulled a Fudgsicle out of the freezer. "Just get me all the *Sex and the City*s they have."

●

Olivia and I were still wrestling with the ice packs when Jeff and Jackson got back with the pizza and videos. "Okay, let's try this," I said. "Hold them on and I'll start wrapping the Ace bandage around your head loosely, then you can slide your hands out."

As soon as Olivia let go, both ice packs slid out and dropped to the floor. Olivia bent down and picked them up. "Can't anyone in this whole house figure this out?" she said. Jeff handed me the pizza boxes and took a step toward her. She turned her back on him. "Never mind, I'll do it myself," she said. She tucked the ice packs and Ace bandage under one arm, then took the video Jackson handed to her. "Just one?" she asked. "Gee, thanks for being so generous. It's a good thing I'm going out tonight." She turned and managed to shuffle out of the kitchen without dropping anything.

Jeff was placing slices of pizza on paper plates. "You don't think she really thinks she's going out tonight, do you?"

I laughed. "I think it's the Percocet talking, but we'd better hide the car keys just in case."

"We could tie her to her bed," Jackson said.

●

I was having the sweetest dream. Olivia and Jackson were little again, and the four of us were at a playground on the edge of a white sand beach. I was pushing Jackson on his swing and Jeff was pushing Olivia on hers, but we were each using only one hand to push. We were holding hands with the other, holding hands and kind of swinging them back and forth, too. Suddenly a car was revving its engine and I thought, *People should be more careful where they park,* and then I heard the side door of our house slam.

I sat up in bed. I looked at the clock. 11:55 P.M. *She wouldn't dare,* I thought. I rolled out of bed and tiptoed into Olivia's room. Her bed was rumpled and empty. Her backpack, laptop even the ice packs and Ace bandage, were gone. I pulled the shade in her window to one side so I could look out at the driveway. Both cars were there. At least she wasn't driving.

I tiptoed back to our bedroom, and shook Jeff by the shoulder. "Yeah, I'm awake," he said.

"Jeff, Olivia's gone," I whispered.

"She must be feeling better," he said. He rolled over and started to snore.

I glared at him for a long moment, then walked around the house checking all the rooms just to be sure she was really gone. I picked up the phone in the kitchen. I was shaking, I noticed.

Olivia answered her cell phone on the third ring. "Hey," she said.

"What do you think you're doing?" I asked.

"Oh, we're just going to a party."

"Olivia, it's midnight."

"That's what time everybody goes out on the weekend." Her speech was muffled but careful, as if she were concentrating on sounding all better. "Well, actually they left at eleven, but then they had to come pick me up."

I concentrated, too, on speaking calmly. "Olivia," I said.

"Don't worry, I won't stay out that long. And I'll sleep really late when I get back to my dorm."

"Turn around and come back here right now."

"I can't. We're almost to Boston. Do you know how much gas it takes to get to Rocky Point?"

I hoped she was lying, because I didn't want to think how fast they were driving if they were almost to Boston. "I mean it," I said.

"Mom, I haven't seen my friends in like forever."

"Olivia."

"What are you, crazy? Do you actually think I'm going to stay in on a Friday night?"

"Olivia."

"I'm sorry, Mom. You just get on my nerves."

"I get on *your* nerves? I love you, Olivia, but . . ."

"Mom, sometimes you love me so much I can't even breathe," she said. Then she hung up.

Long after Olivia hung up on me, I walked around the house in the dark cradling the cordless. It wasn't that it was the worst thing she'd ever said to me. It wasn't even that leaving the house in the middle of the night just hours after surgery was the most foolish thing she'd ever done, or that the rest of us wouldn't eat the food I'd carefully chosen just for her. But my life had been revolving around Olivia's ups and downs for so long, and maybe it just finally hit me: Enough was enough.

19

If you could live your life all over again

- o a. you wouldn't change a thing
- o b. you'd do everything differently
- o c. you'd live it as a blonde
- o d. you'd try being royalty

"Morning," Jeff said as I walked into the kitchen. He was cooking breakfast, a sure sign that he was feeling guilty.

"So she flew the coop, huh?" Jackson said.

"Did you try to wake me up last night, hon?" Jeff asked. I walked silently to the coffeemaker and poured a cup. "Sorry. I must have been exhausted. Long week at work."

"Dad and I are going to take Flighty to the vet this morning. You wouldn't believe how many feathers she's pulled out."

"Hmmm," I said. Jackson and Jeff gave each other a look, and I pretended not to notice. I grabbed the Arts and Living section and sat down at the kitchen table.

"Do you think we should call her, just to make sure she's okay?" Jeff asked. He scooped up two fried eggs with the spatula and put them on a plate.

"Go right ahead," I said. I picked up the paper and my coffee and brought them up to my half of our room.

●

By the time I got to WQBM on Tuesday, I'd managed to work myself up into a pretty good frenzy. How dare Olivia use and abuse me like that? She was lucky to have me for a mother. My own mother would still be telling the story if I'd pulled a stunt like that. Thirty years later, she'd be saying, *Remember that awful night you ran away. What you put your father and me through. I thought you were dead in a ditch.*

"Hey," Olivia said when I walked into the kitchen.

"I thought you were dead in a ditch," I said.

"Well, I'm outta here," Caitlin said. She stood up and headed for the door.

Justin played a drum roll. "Dude, I'm stayin' to watch."

"Justin," Olivia said without taking her eyes off me. "Leave. Now."

As soon as we had the kitchen to ourselves, Olivia said, "What was *that* all about?"

"It seems like I should be the one who gets to ask that question." She had circles under both eyes and a pretty good bruise along one side of her jaw. Her face was still fairly puffy, too. I fought back a rush of maternal sympathy.

"Mom, listen, I'm sorry I went out when you didn't want me to. But, I'm fine so, I mean, get over it."

I tried to remember if I'd ever really glared at my daughter like this before. "Don't worry, honey, I'm over a lot of things."

I'd spent a good part of the weekend making up questions for the show in case we didn't get any callers. I shuffled my purple index cards. "Ten seconds," David's voice said and we listened to a few bars of "Red Rubber Ball." Justin and Caitlin waved from the studio. David and I had agreed that it would be easier to get Olivia going if she didn't have her posse in the same room with her.

"Good afternoon," I said over the fading music. "And welcome to *I'm Rubber, You're Glue*. My name is March Monroe and I'm here with my eighteen-year-old college freshman daughter, Olivia." I glanced up long enough to see Olivia glaring at me for what she would consider a serious oversharing of her personal information. Oh well. "And that's the only thing we're going to agree on for this whole show. So, if you're listening out there, call on in and bounce some questions off us, and we'll see how they stick."

Olivia and I looked at the phone. Nothing. As I always told my clients, being prepared cuts your stress level at least in half. "Okay," I said calmly. "Let's begin with one of the questions our many listeners have mailed in to us. Is that okay with you, Olivia?"

Olivia nodded. I pointed to the microphone. "Yeah, sure," she said.

I'd been hoping for *whatever* or *like I seem to have any choice around here,* but it would have to do. I slid on my reading glasses and continued. "Then here's our first question. 'Dear March and Olivia Monroe of *I'm Rubber, You're Glue* on WQBM Radio. After holding my daughter's hand before, during, and after emergency surgery for her wisdom teeth, she disappeared in the middle of the night with her friends. Do you think that was fair?"

Olivia's mouth dropped open. It must have hurt because she grabbed the bruised side of her jaw with one hand. I winked at her. She hated to be winked at. "Thanks for a great question and I hope you're listening," I said. "Do you want to take it first, Olivia, or shall I?"

"Whatever." Olivia crossed both arms over her chest and slumped down in her chair.

"Okay, then I'll go. I'd have to say that I think that's in-excusable behavior. Not to mention dangerous, since the daughter was probably still weak from the surgery and taking pain medication. And ungrateful. It's completely ungrateful behavior toward someone who sounds like a wonderful mother."

"Oh, puh-lease," Olivia said right into the microphone. "I think the mother should get over herself. It was probably a weekend and the daughter needed to see her friends. I mean, the teeth were out. End of story."

The whiteboard in the studio window caught the corner of my eye. *Phones,* it said. I looked down. Flashing red lights were dancing all over the place. I picked up the receiver and pushed one. "Hi, this is March Monroe and you're on the air. What's your first name, caller?"

"Ann."

"Okay, Ann, what do you have for us?"

"Well. It's my son. Every time he calls it's because he needs money."

Olivia leaned into her microphone. "Your point?" she said.

●

It's not like I expected people to recognize me on the streets. After all, it was only a radio show. But it was mine, or at least half mine, and I thought we'd been pretty damn good at it, even if Olivia no longer appeared to be speaking to me. We'd had callers and everything. Conceivably, hundreds of people had tuned in to it. Dozens anyway.

But, bottom line, whether anyone had heard it or not, there were probably thousands of people, maybe even millions, who'd always wanted their own radio shows, and I was living their dream. Not to mention the fact that I was getting three credits out of the way. I wondered if I could submit tapes of the show instead of writing my internship paper. Or maybe we could even do a show about internships. Call in to tell your own internship stories—the wilder the better. Just bounce 'em right off us and see how they stick. There were so many great possibilities once you got going.

David and I met after the show to discuss some ideas. Just the two of us. We clinked our coffee cups together in the kitchen and congratulated each other. "To *I'm Rubber, You're Glue*," he'd said. "May it bounce higher than the stratosphere. Or at least into syndication."

"And to the idea man behind it all," I said.

"Not to mention the charming woman gracing it with her wit and wisdom," he said. We both laughed and clinked one more time. Then we started brainstorming. We could blanket the greater Boston area with flyers about the show so we could pick up some more listeners. We'd each come up with a list of potential advertisers to approach, and we'd start thinking about other radio stations that might be interested.

It reminded me of how excited Jeff and I used to get over a new idea. When I'd started my party planning business, he'd stayed up late into the night with me planning the fee structure, designing the flyers. He'd even helped me come up with the mailing list and helped address the envelopes. A big part of my decision to go back to school, I suddenly realized, was that Jeff had seemed to be so excited about it in the beginning. Although in hindsight that had more to do with finances than any real interest in a new adventure for me.

It was getting late when I left David and headed for home. The traffic heading south from Boston was light for a change. I barely had to hit the brakes at all, even when Route 3 changed from three lanes to two. Since things were going so well, I decided to get off an exit early and swing by Your Personal Chef to pick up a celebratory dinner. We couldn't really afford it, but so what. I had my own radio show. I found a parking space right away in the trendy little strip mall, which almost never happened.

I pulled the heavy oak door open and, as soon as I stepped inside, I was overwhelmed by how well other people can prepare food. I wanted one of everything, but I settled for a family serving of the Fettuccine with Herbed Shrimp and a tossed baby green salad. Nothing in the world tasted better than a salad that someone else had made. *What the hell,* I thought as I eyed the cooler of overpriced wine and champagne. I cringed at the price of even the cheaper champagnes but bought a bottle anyway because I deserved it. And it would be fun to celebrate with Jeff.

It would be embarrassing to actually admit it, but when I paid for my purchases I was half hoping the woman behind the counter would recognize my voice. "Good afternoon," I said. It was technically evening, but that's the way I'd greeted everyone on the air, so I thought it might give me the best chance for recognition.

"Is there anything else you'd like?" she asked. Maybe she'd been working all day and missed the show. She was about my age, though, and would probably relate to what I was going through.

"Thanks, but I think that'll do it. I'm celebrating having my very own radio show on WQBM. It's so exciting, just the way you'd think it would be."

It wasn't like I expected her to ask me for an autograph or anything, but I thought she should have at least managed a polite congratulations. But all I got was a bored look and, "We're having a special on the chocolate mousse today," which was probably something she would have said to anyone.

●

I stood behind the couch in the family room. Jeff and Jackson were watching a show I couldn't identify on Comedy Central. Neither of them seemed to want to tear themselves away from it long enough to answer my question. "You missed it again?" I repeated.

"Sorry, hon."

"Sorry, Mom."

They both started to laugh their identical laughs. I usually liked the way they laughed, both the sameness and the distinctly male sound, but right now it sounded like kind of a cross between a bray and a guffaw, something you'd hear from a couple of donkeys. I turned and walked back out to the kitchen. Okay, maybe I stomped.

I unpacked the Your Personal Chef bag and placed the container of Fettuccine with Herbed Shrimp on the counter. I tucked the bottle of champagne way in the back of the refrigerator so I wouldn't be tempted to conk Jeff over the head with it. I made a fair amount of noise as I opened drawers and rattled silverware and clomped back and forth to the dining room as I set the table.

"God, that was funny," Jeff said a few minutes later. "You should have watched." I noticed he hadn't ventured all the way into the kitchen. He had great instincts.

"God, I was good," I said. "You should have listened." I bent over and pulled the fettuccine out of the oven, where it had been staying warm.

"Can I help with anything, Mom?" Jackson asked.

"No, thanks," I said. "I'm all set." I carried the fettuccine past them into the dining room and put it down next to the salad and rolls. I pulled out my chair and sat down. My posture felt self-righteous even to me.

"Mmm," Jeff said. "This is a treat." He helped himself to a huge serving of the creamy pasta. "So, did you and Olivia get some good calls?"

"Mm-hmm," I said. Jackson was fishing for the shrimp and eating them first.

"And how was school today?" Jeff asked.

"Okay," Jackson said.

"Great, but I meant your mother. How was school, hon?"

I stared at him. "I didn't have school today," I said.

Jeff took a sip of milk, a few bites of salad. "So," he said. "Homework night tonight, then."

"I don't feel like doing my homework," I said. "I'm not even sure I feel like being in school."

Jackson swallowed down some roll. "Whoa, Mom, bad attitude. You'd ground me for that one."

"And don't forget it," I said, forcing myself to smile. I twirled some fettuccine around my fork.

"Just be careful you don't lose your focus, March. You've got a lot on your plate."

I looked down at my plate. Greasy pasta swam in liquid fat. I stood up. "Excuse me," I said.

Jeff followed me into the kitchen. "I really am sorry I missed the show again," he said. He put his arms around me and gave me a kiss. "I thought of a great name for it though. *Dueling Coeds.*"

"A little late, don't you think?" I said. I twisted away and put my plate in the dishwasher. "We've already had a name for two shows now."

20

> When you're feeling stuck, the best thing to do
> is
>
> ○ a. try something new
> ○ b. try not to think about it
> ○ c. find someone else to blame
> ○ d. develop multiple personalities

David Callahan had been busy. "What?" I asked again after he explained it the second time. I eyed two red and white polka-dot dresses he'd just carried in from his car. Even under their plastic bags they were bright. I pulled the plastic up over them. The polka dots on both were roughly the same size as tennis balls, but I could see now that the outfits weren't exactly identical. One was a two piece that had a smallish top with a cutout back and a very short, low-slung flouncy skirt, and the other was kind of a *Stepford Wives* sundress with a little jacket. It seemed safe to assume that one would be mine.

"How'd you know our sizes?" I asked to stall for time. I'd had a lot of fantasies about David Callahan, but this wasn't one of them. What I really wanted to say was, *You don't actually think we're going to wear those, do you?* Maybe I could just stand back and wait for Olivia to get me off the hook. Olivia wouldn't be caught dead in one of those dresses.

"I asked the receptionist. She knew right away." David hung the dresses carefully on the back of the studio door. He turned and gave me a big smile. He was standing there like a puppy waiting to be told he's a good boy. Just this morning on my way to work I'd imagined us off in Tuscany together, sitting across from each other at a table at an outdoor cafe, sipping drinks and hanging on each other's every word. Both of our spouses were somehow out of the picture so there was no guilt involved. The details of that were vague. They were either in comas or had amnesia, or maybe one was in a coma and the other had amnesia since they'd be unlikely to have the same thing at the same time.

There were no polka dots anywhere in that fantasy. "Really. Well," I said.

"So, what do you think? Is this a great idea or is this a great idea?"

I wrestled with my thoughts while David watched me attentively. I could tell it meant a lot to him. And even if I said yes, Olivia would be sure to veto it anyway. "Okay," I said finally. "But you have to explain it to Olivia."

David wasn't gone for long, and when he came back he brought all three interns with him.

"Dude," Justin said. "That's a lot of spots."

"Red rubber balls," David said. "Get it?" I could tell he was nervous because he rubbed the palms of his hands up and down on the thighs of his jeans a few times, then checked his watch.

"Ohmigod," Olivia said. She lifted one of the hangers off the door. I slouched down in a chair and got ready for the fireworks. "Wow. Beyoncé had this outfit."

I looked at my daughter. She was fingering the polka-dotted fabric with what looked like reverence. She hadn't liked an outfit chosen by an adult since she was six.

"Dude, her backup dancers had it, too," Justin said. "It was post–Destiny's Child, early Beyoncé. They even wore them on the *Today Show.*"

Caitlin said, "This outfit completely rocks. Can I borrow it sometime if I'm really careful, Olivia?"

The worst thing about teenagers was that you couldn't even count on them to be negative. David and I looked at each other. He smiled. I shrugged. I'd been so sure she was going to hate it. David turned back to Olivia. "Sorry," he said. "It's only borrowed for the afternoon. The tags stay on. And the photographer will be here in a minute, so we better get moving."

"Okay," Caitlin said. "But I think I should at least get to try it on after Olivia. I promise not to sweat on it or anything."

●

"So," Olivia said. "We're actually going to be on the billboard? The one you can see from the expressway. The great big one?"

"Apparently so," I said. "The billboard's on WQBM property and the station owns it. Sometimes it's leased but not right now. So David talked George Dickerman into letting us use it. David's making a deal with a graphics company that owes the station money, so they're doing the billboard design for our show, and they're sending a photographer."

I handed Olivia the bottom half of her outfit. She held it at hip level, and looked down while she swung it back and forth as if it were dancing. She looked up. "You know," she said, "you sure talk about *David* a lot. Does he know about Dad?"

"Know what about Dad?"

"That you're married to him?"

"Of course he does," I said. Olivia stepped into her skirt, then slipped her jeans out from under it and threw them up over one of the stall doors. I handed her the top part and she disappeared inside the stall. Olivia wasn't usually this modest in front of me, and I wondered if she might be hiding a newly acquired tattoo or something. I hoped never to find out if she was.

I brought my outfit into another stall to change. It had been decades since I'd changed in a bathroom stall, and they'd once seemed roomier. I hadn't really thought about the germs back then, either. I managed to get the sundress on without dipping it into the toilet. It was a perfect fit, which meant I'd underestimated the receptionist on some level, I supposed. I kicked my shoes off long enough to get my pants off, trying not to think about whether you could catch plantar warts through your socks. I carried the jacket back out with me.

Olivia was standing sideways and inspecting herself in the mirror. "Honey," I said, "don't you think you should pull the skirt up a little higher?"

"It's supposed to be like this." A good five or six inches of my daughter's abdomen was exposed. I didn't like the look in the WQBM bathroom, and I imagined I'd like it a lot less gracing a billboard on the side of the highway.

I chose my words carefully. "It's just that . . ."

Olivia glared at me. "I don't know what your problem is."

"But . . ."

Olivia turned so she could see the profile of her abdomen from the other direction. "I don't want to talk about it," she said. She gave herself one last look in the mirror, then walked out of the bathroom.

I put my little polka-dot jacket on and looked at myself in the mirror. The dots were a bit much and the style was in-your-face Doris Day, but red was a good color on me.

●

"How about," Olivia said, "if I'm on one side of the billboard and she's on the other?"

David laughed. We were outside looking up at the peeling billboard. "That's not a bad idea," he said. "But there's no guarantee everyone will pass it in both directions."

"Dude," Justin said, "their teeth are going to be about a foot long on that thing. How do you get the picture up there any-way?"

"I've seen them do it," Caitlin said. "It's just like wallpaper."

"I think," the photographer said, pointing to an open area by the side of the road, "right over there is our best bet. The light's good and they'll drop the background in afterward anyway." There was nothing about the photographer, besides the fact that she had a camera, that inspired confidence. She looked bored and wore a rumpled black jogging suit that ex-pressed neither creativity nor attention to detail.

Olivia and I walked over to the designated spot and stood side by side. "Wouldn't it be better to do this in your studio?" Olivia asked the photographer.

"I prefer natural light." She held up a light meter and moved it around half-heartedly. "And I'm temporarily with-out a studio."

"Okay," David said. "How about back to back, with your arms crossed. Like you're not really speaking to each other."

"That'll be a stretch," Olivia said.

The photographer crouched down. David, Caitlin, and Justin looked over the photographer's shoulder. "Wait a minute," David said. He walked over and put his hands on my elbows and lifted them up slightly. "There, that's good. Turn your head just a little more. Perfect."

I gave him what I hoped was a brave smile.

"Hey," he said. "Are you sure you're okay with this?"

"On a scale of one to ten?" I noticed he was still holding on to my elbows, and he was looking at me with real concern. "It'll probably be fine, but, well, it's about this dress. Are you sure I look okay?"

He laughed. He moved his hands up to my shoulders and looked into my eyes. "You look absolutely gorgeous," he said softly.

As he walked away, I heard Olivia mumble something behind me. "Excuse me?" I said.

"Dad's cuter," she said.

"What's that supposed to mean?" I asked.

"Mom, I know you. You wouldn't let just anyone dress you in polka dots."

We'd been leaning back against each other, and I took a step away from her, which made Olivia start to fall backward. "Hey," she yelled.

A lesser mother might have let her fall, but I took a quick step back and turned and glared at the camera. Olivia must have, too, because David said, "Great. That's it."

"You sure?" the photographer asked. "Shouldn't we make them say cheese or something?"

21

College the second time around can give you

- ○ a. a better-paying job
- ○ b. improved self-esteem
- ○ c. access to a new world
- ○ d. a bad case of hives

I waited in dread while my Quantum Physics and You professor passed back our exams. One by one she read off the names, the appropriate students raised their hands, and she walked over and handed them their tests. "Nice job," she said occasionally. There were only about thirty or so people in the class, but I wished there were a thousand so we'd run out of time before she could give me mine. Then, after a while, I hoped mine would be next, just to get it over with.

Every test I'd ever done poorly on in my entire life came back to haunt me, along with everything else I'd ever failed at. Like the time I'd tried out for chorus in sixth grade and that nasty music teacher actually cringed when I tried to hit a high note. Or junior year in high school when Mark Fitzpatrick asked another girl to the prom instead of me.

"March Monroe," the professor said. I forced myself to smile and say thank you when she handed me my test. I looked down as casually as I could manage: 73. Even with a 106 average in Greek civ thanks to some extra credit questions, and an A on the paper I'd just gotten back in my English novel class, this would kill my GPA. I felt an irrational jolt of anger toward Etta and Jeff for not doing a better job of helping me, but let it go quickly. It wasn't their fault I wasn't capable of higher level thought.

I'd be horrified to hear someone else have even half this much self-pity. I'd lecture my kids out of it and coach my clients into a better attitude. Frustrated, I crumpled the test into a tight ball and stuffed it into my bag. God, I'd studied so hard. I knew I was completely overreacting, but hot tears made my moisturizer run into my eyes anyway. The moisturizer burned, and that made my eyes tear even more. I reached around blindly in my bag and found a tissue.

"March, dear, wait up." I wiped my eyes and pretended not to hear Etta, then practically ran up the stairs from the dank cellar classroom and out into the dreary afternoon. It would be dark at this hour before I knew it. And after that would come snow, cold, dark days and, the way things were going, probably my first bout of seasonal affective disorder.

I trudged across the tiny campus, then plunged down another set of stairs to a cheerless waiting room. I had plenty of time while waiting to see my *individualized academic counselor* to do the math. Even if I got a 100 on the next test, with a 71 on my first test and a 73 on this one, it would still only bring my average up to an 81.1. Of course, that was assuming I was smart enough to average three numbers together correctly.

The door opened and a very young student walked out. My child counselor stood in the doorway. "Next," she said, motioning me into her office. Her tiny square teeth reminded me of the Chiclets gum I used to chew as a teenager.

I sat in the molded Formica chair across from her desk, remembering how optimistic I'd been last time I was here. Okay, sure, I was a little bit annoyed about the internship requirement then, but at least I was still hopeful about my intelligence. "What can I do for you?" my counselor asked as she reached into a drawer of her desk and pulled out a bottle of clear nail polish.

"Well," I said, watching her apply the nail polish to the tip of a nail. "I think I might need to drop a class."

"Sorry. Tomorrow's the last day," she said without looking up. "You have to get the slip signed by the instructor by then. And then by the other instructor, since I assume you'll want to add another class because it's against our policy to give refunds after the first week of classes. So just make up your mind and, you know, pick another one."

I swallowed hard. "Well, I'm feeling very conflicted about it."

"Sorry. What class?"

"Quantum Physics and You."

"Don't worry, everybody who's not a total brainiac drops that one."

I shook my head. "It's just that I feel like I should be better than that."

She twisted the top back on the nail polish and smiled at

me. "Rocks for Jocks," she said. "You can't lose. It's mostly field trips." She extended her hand to check out her nailwork. "Oh, sorry. Technically, I'm supposed to call it Geology 101."

On my way out of the office, drop/ad slip in hand, I promised myself that I was going to hang on to my Quantum Physics and You textbook and, as soon as I had an extra minute, I was going to read every last page of it. Maybe I'd even retake it down the road.

Etta was waiting for me in the hallway. She was wearing a hot-pink jogging suit with matching Keds. "What's wrong, dear?" she asked. "You look like you could use a good stiff drink."

We decided to get the driving out of the way first, then meet at Water's Edge since it was about halfway between Etta's and my houses. I found an empty booth way in the back of the bar. The booths at Water's Edge had been salvaged from an old ferry. They were heavy and high, and the wood had been painted many times over the years. The new owners had given them a coat of soft green paint. You could feel uneven layers of other paints underneath, worn or sanded away in places, and every chip exposed a tiny rainbow of color.

Before anyone came over to wait on me, Etta arrived in a flash of pink and sat down on the other side of the booth. She pushed up the sleeves of her jacket and gave the table between us a single brisk slap with both palms. "Now, my dear March, I bet you've never even tried a milk chocolate martini."

I tried to sound enthusiastic. "A chocolate martini?"

"No, chocolate martinis are out. Milk chocolate martinis are in. At least at my bridge club."

"What's in a milk chocolate martini?" I asked, even though they'd probably been around for years. Not only was I sorely lacking in intelligence, but even my seventy-something-year-old friend was hipper than I was.

Etta counted it off on her fingers. "Stoli vanilla vodka, Godiva liqueur, and cream." She leaned over the booth and lowered her voice. "Though I must admit that, as a drink, I find it vastly inferior to the Brandy Alexander of my day."

A waiter dressed like a pirate came over and Etta ordered for us. As he walked away, she brushed a white curl from her forehead and whispered, "I just love a man in tights, don't you, March?"

I forced myself to smile. "Absolutely."

Etta folded her hands, and her rings poked through the basketweave of her fingers. "When my husband was alive, he had the most divine calf muscles. So what seems to be the problem, dear?"

"I think I'm going to have to drop Quantum Physics and You, and it's making me feel like a complete failure." I looked over my shoulder, then back at Etta. "I got a seventy-three on the exam we got back today."

"And I got a ninety-four. So what do I win?"

"What do you mean?"

"I mean what's the contest? You passed and I passed, and we're both beyond the stage where anyone is giving us nickels for our A's."

I took a sip of my water and thought about it. "I think the price has gone up. When my son, Jackson, was in first grade, he said a boy in his class got a twenty-dollar bill for each A. And once a girl in my daughter Olivia's class got a car for a good report card. Or at least that's what Olivia said. I never quite bought that one."

Etta reached out and patted my hand. "The other day," she said, "I was watching that fine young Dr. Bill's show while I walked on my treadmill. My sister, Martha, just got me hooked on that one, though you won't catch her moving one muscle while she watches, I'll guarantee you that."

Our pirate server came back and placed an oversized martini glass in front of each of us. Decadent chocolate curls wrapped themselves around blue-and-white-striped straws. "So," I said to Etta as soon as he'd walked away. "Do we drink these or just pour them directly onto our cellulite?"

"Everything in moderation, my dear. Everything in moderation. But back to Bill. He was counseling this very good-looking couple who sat around beautifully dressed and coifed all day, boring each other to tears by being so perfect. He told them to let their hair down, or maybe it was mess it up a little, and by the end of the show he had the husband juggling tennis balls in the middle of a mall and the wife dancing on top of her parked car."

I stirred my martini. The chocolate curl broke apart and fell in. "I dance on my car all the time," I said, hoping I didn't sound defensive.

Etta broke a tiny piece of chocolate off her straw and popped it into her mouth. "Be that as it may, tell me, dear, do you think you have a tad too much on your plate?"

"Who doesn't," I said. "It's like the minute you think you're going to get some free time, something rushes in to fill it."

"Fortunately for me, overscheduling is a younger woman's disease, and probably far worse now than when I was your age." Etta removed the straw from her martini and placed it on her cocktail napkin, then leaned forward for a sip. When she lifted up her head, she had a tiny dot of chocolate on the tip of her nose. I reached across the booth for a napkin and handed it to her.

"Thanks, dear," she said. She dabbed at her nose, then scrunched up the napkin and tucked it under one of the cuffs of her pink jacket. "We didn't overthink things as much back in those days, either. We simply didn't have as many choices. Your world is more complicated, I'm afraid."

I picked up my glass in one hand, but had to rush my other hand up to steady it before the drink sloshed over the sides. "So, you always just kept things simple?"

"Good God, no. Once Edward went to school, I worked part-time in my husband's law office. And I can clearly remember finding myself on umpteen committees with barely a minute to stay on top of my own life." She looked me directly in the eyes and smiled. "Do you want to know the secret it took me years to discover?"

"Oh, you have no idea," I said. I wrestled my milk chocolate martini back down on the table so I could take a sip through the straw. If you factored out the calories, and the way your arteries were clogging with every sip, it was delicious.

"To the extent that it's possible, choose the things you enjoy and let the rest of them go."

I wondered how many clients I'd said similar things to. "You're right, Etta. You're absolutely right."

We finished our drinks, paid our check, and stood up when the waiter delivered the take-out food I'd ordered. I leaned over and hugged Etta. She smelled like talcum powder and Godiva chocolate. "If I decide to drop Quantum Physics and You, can we still hang out together sometimes?"

"I'd be thrilled and honored, March. But get your ducks in a row first."

22

Every day it's important to make a list of

- ☐ a. things you have to be grateful for
- ☐ b. things that drive you crazy
- ☐ c. things you have to do before you go to sleep
- ☐ d. things you should make lists of

Jeff took a couple of bites of the fish and chips I'd brought home with me from Water's Edge, then washed them down with a sip of the Smuttynose beer we'd started buying because we liked the name. The fish and chips weren't as good as they used to be. Just about everybody used cod instead of haddock now, and gone were the days of massive hunks of fried fish. Now it was mostly french fries, and I'd somehow become one of those people who remembered the good old days.

"So," I said. "Where did you say Jackson is?"

"At Brian's house with Zack. Either that or at Zack's house with Brian."

I felt a flash of impatience. "Any idea how we'll get him back?"

Jeff gave me a look I didn't think I completely deserved. "I've got it under control, March. They're working on a history project and I'm picking him up at 8:30."

"So . . . what? You'll just drive to one house, and if he's not there, you'll go to the other?"

We looked at each other. It wasn't a very long look, but long enough for me to decide to back off. It was quite possible that the couples who stayed married did so because they'd learned to recognize that one-more-word-and-we'll-be-in-a-big-fight look. Jeff took a sip of his beer. I took a large drink of water, trying to flush my milk chocolate martini out of my system. "So, how was school?" Jeff asked finally.

"Not so hot. That's why I went out with my friend Etta. I did really bad on a Quantum Physics and You exam, so I was going to drop it and add another class, but now I'm thinking I'll lower my expectations a little and just try to pass."

"Maybe you should put in a little more time studying."

"Excuse me?"

"I think if you put in an hour a day, maybe sit down right after dinner . . ."

It seemed awfully soon to be having that look again, but there it was. Our eyes locked and all the things that aggravated us about each other stretched between us, just asking to be pointed out. I waited for Jeff to back off. He took the final bite of his fish, then one of coleslaw. "It's just," he said, "that you sure seem to be losing your focus awful quickly."

I squeezed some more lemon on my fish, then looked up again. "Maybe I'm finding out that school isn't what I was looking for."

"I thought you really wanted to go back to school."

"You know, Jeff, everything isn't always the way it looks on paper. I thought it was going to be great, but to tell you the truth, I'm having a lot more fun at the radio station. Did I tell you Olivia and I are going to be on a billboard ad?"

"Well, maybe you can take a broadcasting class next semester."

"I suppose I could do that. But I already have my own show, or at least half a show. You know, I think you just want the school thing to work because it was your idea."

"What's that supposed to mean?"

"Jeff, come on. I'm too tired to fight. I'm going to finish the semester. Who knows, maybe I'm still getting used to it." Jeff took another sip of his beer, and I squeezed some more lemon onto what was left of my fish. "So, anything interesting happen at work today?"

●

Clark and Hillary were sitting on the steps waiting for me when I pulled into their driveway. I'd scheduled Ahndrayuh's final session late to make sure Clark would be home from school.

Clark ran down and opened the car door for me. "Thanks, Clark," I said. "You are a gentleman and a prince."

Hillary was right behind him. She took her thumb out of her mouth. "Me, too," she said.

"Absolutely," I said.

"She can't be. She's a girl. She has to be a lady and a queen."

"Or a princess," I said.

"Princess," Hillary said.

That much decided, we started walking toward the front door. Clark bent down and picked a couple of blades of grass. "My mother said to tell you she's not coming out."

I stopped walking. "What?"

Clark pushed his glasses farther up his nose. "Dad says it's a good thing she's so pretty."

"I'm pretty," Hillary said.

I put my hands on her shoulders. "And you're smart and you can be anything you want to be. Come on, you two, of course she'll come out."

Clark rang the bell. "Can't we just open it?" I asked.

"It locks automatically," Clark said.

"What about the back door?"

"That one, too." He rang the doorbell again, then gave his glasses another push toward his face.

Hillary squatted down. She took her thumb out of her mouth, lifted the shell off a small stone turtle, and placed it on the porch. She took a key out of the turtle's insides and handed it to Clark.

Just as Clark got the key into the lock, Ahndrayuh opened the door. "Oh," she said. "I wondered who that was." She tucked some hair behind an ear.

"Ahndrayuh," I said. "You know I'm here for your final session. You have to come out. Now."

Clark and Hillary were watching us like we were a cartoon. Ahndrayuh evened out the cuffs on her blouse, then looked at me with her turquoise eyes. "If I don't come out, you can't quit on me."

I crossed my arms over my chest. "Ahndrayuh, listen to me."

Ahndrayuh covered her ears with her hands. She closed her eyes. "Watermelon," she said. "Cucumber. Baby mesclun." She removed one hand long enough to shut the door in our faces.

"You say those when you don't want to hear what the other person is saying," Clark explained.

"You're very smart," I said. "And very handsome," I added to keep things balanced with his sister.

"I'm pretty," Hillary said.

I could have just turned around and left, I knew that. Or I could have kept my finger on the doorbell until Ahndrayuh came out. Instead, I decided to take the kids for a walk. There couldn't have been much more than an hour left before dark, tops. The sky had gotten cloudy, too, making it look and feel like a real autumn day. All the trees were late this year. The leaves of a big sugar maple that had somehow managed to live through the building of this subdivision had just started to change color.

The owners of one of the oversized Colonials way at the end of the cul-de-sac had placed a row of tiny pumpkins across the railing of a second floor Juliet balcony. A ray of sunshine suddenly broke through the clouds and shone directly on the house, lighting it up like a religious painting. I stopped walking and pointed. "Look," I said to the kids. "Isn't that beautiful?"

Clark let go of my hand to adjust his glasses. "But those poor people who live there," he said. "The light is always shining on their TV."

These children need me, I thought. Even after I finally got rid of their mother, I'd have to find a way to stay in their lives. I held on to Hillary's hand a little tighter, and reached with my other hand to pat Clark's silky hair.

Just as we were heading back down the street, a red jeep pulled into their driveway. "Jenny!" Clark yelled. Hillary yanked her hand out of mine.

"Who's Jenny?" I asked as the kids ran away from me.

Clark turned around long enough to say, "Jenny is our other baby-sitter. She's our favorite."

Ahndrayuh came out of her house with an impossibly tiny bag hanging from her shoulder. She held the door open while Jenny and the children who'd been so attached to me moments before went inside. "Not that this is our last session," Ahndrayuh said. "But I want to make sure I get the dress for my friend's wedding just in case. Remember? That was our goal."

It was amazing the way an Ahndrayuh could just kind of drag you along in her wake. She didn't think the rules applied to her, and every time you'd try to say no to her, your own good manners would get in your way. *Just say no,* I coached myself.

"I'm curious," I said. "How did you get the baby-sitter so fast?"

"I just called her on her cell phone. I pay her double what everybody else does, so she always comes."

I hoped I was maintaining some semblance of control by opening the door to my vehicle instead of hers. "You should have checked with me first," I said.

"Oh sorry. I always do that. I just don't seem to recognize boundaries. It's like I don't know where I end and other people begin. It pretty much feels like it's all me."

I put my car into reverse and started backing out of the driveway. "Well, maybe that's a good goal for you, Ahndrayuh. You know, after we find you a dress for the wedding, you could work on boundaries."

"Why? Wow. Even though this is a van, I still feel so short. That's why I love my Suburban, because I'm above everyone else. You know, March, what I really wish is that you were my mother."

"I don't think I'm old enough to be your mother, Ahndrayuh."

"Of course you are."

"What's your mother like?" I asked just to keep her from doing the math out loud.

Ahndrayuh half-reclined across the seat and leaned against the passenger door. "Busy. All I remember is that she was always getting ready for the next day. And she never baked, so I never knew you could bake things at home. I thought cookies only came in boxes."

"So do you bake a lot at home now?"

"How could I? No one ever taught me."

I could feel a headache coming on. I reminded myself that if I survived the next little bit of time, I'd never have to see Ahndrayuh again. I could change our phone number if I had to. I decided to take her to an upscale little clump of shops called Commodore Court because it was nearby and expensive.

We pulled into a parking space. The window boxes on all of the stores looked like small rowboats that had crashed sideways into the buildings. Buoys were impaled in clusters on vacant wall space, and ceramic sea captains perched atop tall posts and peered out over the brass lanterns they held in their hands. It seemed to me that the trendier they tried to become, the more towns like Rocky Point, with their natural seaside charm, risked turning into a parody of themselves.

We followed carved wooden signs shaped like seagulls to a boutique that, despite its unfortunate name, She Shell, carried enough fashionable and pricey clothes to be right up Ahndrayuh's alley. As soon as we got inside, I started pulling dresses off the rack. I waved the salesperson away, and handed the hangers to Ahndrayuh. Then I plopped myself in an overstuffed chair outside the dressing room and vowed to tell her how perfect the first dress she tried on looked.

I didn't even have to exaggerate because it did. As did the second dress . . . and the third. I wondered if things looked that good on me at her age and, if so, why I'd never appreciated it. Maybe when I was Etta's age, I'd look back and think I looked great now.

Eventually, Ahndrayuh bought two dresses, one that she liked the best and a second one in case she changed her mind. Finally, we were back in her driveway and I was saying goodbye firmly and for good. "So, that's it," I said, enunciating clearly. "Mission accomplished."

"Well," Ahndrayuh said, "if you can't still be my directionality coach, maybe I could take a class with you."

"Gee," I said. "I'm not even sure school is working out." I hoped that didn't make it sound like I was going to have some free time opening up. "Plus I'm just so busy these days. Did I tell you my daughter and I have our own radio show?"

"Oh, you lucky ducks. Do you think I could be on it with you? Just once?"

It didn't surprise me in the least that Ahndrayuh hadn't even bothered to ask what the show was about. I checked my watch. "Will you look at the time. Anyway, it's a call-in show, Ahndrayuh. So all you have to do is listen in and when you have something to say, you can, you know, just pick up the phone and call. It'll feel like you're still seeing me once in a while." I leaned across her and opened the passenger door. "Well, I'm leaving now. Good-bye. Take care of yourself and say bye to the kids for me."

"What if I just refused to get out of your car?"

There's a time in your life when you finally realize that you can't be all things to all people. You don't even have to pretend to like all people, and you certainly don't have to let them guilt you into doing what you don't want to do.

"Good-bye, Ahndrayuh," I said firmly, giving her just a little shove.

23

Getting back in touch with what you're good at
means

○ a. defining good

○ b. finding a spare moment to think

○ c. defining think

○ d. remembering what the question was in the
first place

I'd never really stopped to think about what my kids would say to other people when they looked back on my mothering. And especially what they might say to their own kids someday. But, after our last session, I found myself wondering, what if Olivia and Jackson didn't think any more of me than Ahndrayuh did of her mother?

I raced up and down the aisles of Stop & Shop with my cart, trying to remember what you put in brownies when you made them from scratch. I was pretty sure I had it covered, but I threw in a couple packages of Duncan Hines Double

Fudge brownie mix just in case. I could always ditch the evidence.

Jackson was sitting at the kitchen table eating a bowl of frozen yogurt when I kicked the kitchen door open so I didn't have to put the bags down first. "Wow," he said. "Groceries. Is it someone's birthday?"

"Cute," I said. "Go get the other bags, Jackson, okay?" I remembered that he might well be recording this event and rating my performance. I leaned over and gave him a motherly kiss on his forehead. "Hope I got all your favorites, honey."

Jackson walked past me and I squinted at his ice cream bowl. Crumbled chocolate chip cookies and pieces of fruit roll-up all but obscured the vanilla frozen yogurt I'd bought because it was healthier than ice cream. I cut up a Granny Smith apple and casually placed the slices beside the bowl.

Jackson came back in with five or six plastic grocery bags looped over his wrists. He lifted both arms up so the bags landed on the counter, then stepped backward until his hands were free. He sat down again and dipped an apple slice into his frozen yogurt, as if the apple had been there all along. I wondered if I should point out my fruit-slicing so he'd remember it warmly for posterity, or if it would just make him stop eating the apple.

I put away the groceries that needed to be refrigerated and shoved the rest down to one end of the counter. I reached up to the cookbook shelf, pulled down my old Betty Crocker cookbook, and released a small cloud of dust when I opened it. I found the recipe for brownies and grabbed my old Pyrex mixing bowl.

"If you like these, I think I'll make a second batch to freeze for you and your friends," I said as I cracked two eggs into the bowl. "Maybe Brian and Zack can sleep over this weekend." I was feeling so June Cleaver. I wondered if I still had any aprons hanging around anywhere.

Jackson lifted his head up from his bowl. "Nope. It's Brian's weekend with his father and Zack has to go to Martha's Vineyard with his parents."

I fished a couple of stray eggshell pieces out with a spoon. "Martha's Vineyard. That's rough."

"He hates it. He says it's like being on Alcatraz. Once you're on you can't get off."

I could feel a lecture on entitlement coming over me. I knew this would be counterproductive in terms of my quest for being remembered as a wonderful mother, so I changed the subject. "So, how was school today?"

"It sucked. Can I get a car?"

"Jackson, you can't even get your license for two more years." I pulled out two squares of baker's chocolate from the box and unwrapped their paper covering. The dark chocolate had a white cast over it. It had probably been sitting on the shelf for years waiting for some sucker like me to decide to bake again. I opened the trash compactor, and threw the whole box in. I tore open the Duncan Hines mix and poured it on top of the eggs.

Jackson didn't seem to notice. "I know that," he said. "I don't need to drive it. I just need to have it."

"Why?" I added water and oil, stirred forty times, sprayed a square baking pan with Pam, poured the batter in, popped the whole thing in the oven, and set the timer for twenty-seven minutes.

"Well, because then I'd still be socially inept but at least I'd be socially inept with a car."

I pulled out the chair across from Jackson and sat down. "Oh, honey, who called you socially inept?"

"No one, Mom. You're missing the point."

"But, Jackson, you're not socially inept at all. You're really good with people. And you're funny and handsome . . ."

"Mom, don't you have homework to do or something? I'll watch the brownies."

So I let him take over my brownies and went off to do my homework. The hardest part about bringing up your kids to be strong and independent was that then you had to let them be.

●

By the time I headed back to WQBM again, Jackson was ready to host his own baking show. He'd made the second box of brownies I'd bought, then moved on to Congo Bars, Rice Krispies squares (though technically those were no-bake), then back to brownies again. Most people don't realize how much some fourteen-year-old boys enjoy baking, and what a particularly useful skill it is to have once they've eaten all the prepared food in the house.

He'd baked an extra batch of double-chocolate brownies for me to take in to Olivia. I pulled off the expressway at the exit before the station, so I didn't know the billboard was already up. I walked down the hallway with my paper plate full of brownies, looking for Olivia and the other interns.

"Dude," Justin said, as he walked toward me with Olivia and Caitlin. "We're going to go check out the billboard. You and Liv are like on it already."

I was focused on the brownies. I peeled back the plastic wrap and held them out.

"What is that?" Olivia said. "You never bake."

"Jackson made them for you."

"Oh, that's so sweet. No thanks. I'm saving my calories for this weekend." She put her hands behind her back and walked past me.

I held them out to Caitlin and she shook her head and said, "Wait up, Olivia."

"Justin?" I asked.

"Dude, I think my metabolism is slowing down. I'm not even hungry. But, like save me one, okay?"

The green light was on over the studio door, so I knocked once and opened it. I held out the plate toward David.

He smiled. "Wow, real brownies," he said. "My wife never bakes." I wondered whether I should confess that I hadn't exactly baked them either. He reached out and grabbed one and bit off half of it. "Don't say it. I know. I could bake, too."

"I wasn't going to say that. What I was going to say was how did you get the billboard done already?"

He finished chewing before he answered. His eyes were so blue when he chewed. "Well, the graphics company put a rush on it, and there's permanent scaffolding built in around the billboard, so all I had to do was find an out-of-work wallpaperer who wasn't afraid of heights, and promise him free ads for his business. Piece of cake. These are amazing, by the way."

"Thanks," I said. He had a brownie crumb on his cheek and, without thinking, I leaned forward and brushed it off.

His eyes were pretty blue even when he wasn't chewing. They were looking right at me, and I could feel myself starting to blush. Or maybe it was that first hot flash brought on by the stress of being in a small, closed studio that suddenly felt like a hotel room. *Blush*, I thought. *Hot flash. No, blush. Wait, I really think it's a hot flash.*

"What are you thinking about?" David Callahan asked.

"Nothing," I said. Why is it that when you fantasize about moments like this you always say something so much wittier? The guy says, *What are you thinking about?* And you look him in the eyes and say, *What do you think I'm thinking about?* And he laughs and gives you a knowing look and takes another step toward you, and you flip your hair back coquettishly, whatever that means, and take a step toward him . . .

I turned and took a couple of steps away, which brought me to the other end of the studio. I concentrated on putting the brownies down between a couple of CD cases on the counter without dropping them. "Well," I said, pushing the door open and taking a big gulp of the hallway air. "See ya. I'm going to go check out the billboard."

"Wait." David was suddenly walking down the hallway beside me. "You didn't see it from the road on the way here? I had this great picture of how surprised you were going to be when you saw it."

"No, the exit comes up before the station when you're heading north. But maybe that's a good thing. I might have caused an accident. You know, from the shock." I laughed, and even to me it sounded like I was trying too hard.

David turned his head toward me. "I guess I should have called you last night. Not that I know your number or what town you live in."

I smiled. "I'm sure Dickerman has it on file."

"Yeah, like he'd recognize a file if it bit him." I wasn't the only one who sounded like I was trying too hard. David stopped walking and looked at his watch. "We have enough time before the show. Come on, you have to see it from the road to get the full effect."

My heart skipped a beat, then caught up. A car was even smaller than the studio. "Sure," I said, trying to sound casual. "But let's take the other interns with us."

●

I told David that the other interns had gone outside to look at the billboard. He nodded, as if it were perfectly reasonable that we'd go find them to ask them to go for a ride to look at the billboard some more. Maybe I wasn't the only one who felt the need for some chaperones.

The station grounds weren't exactly vast, and we could see the interns as soon as we opened the front door. It felt like a longer walk than it was, though, since I was trying not to look at either David or the billboard, which didn't leave a whole lot of options. I pretty much stared at my feet until we joined the others where they were standing in front of the billboard. I took a deep breath and looked up. It was tough enough to look at myself in a full-length mirror some days. A billboard was beyond daunting. Giant-sized versions of Olivia and me, back to back, covered in red polka dots, hands on our hips and heads turned, glared at the camera. I'M RUBBER, YOU'RE GLUE, it said. CALL IN THURSDAYS AT 3 AND BOUNCE YOUR IDEAS OFF US.

"Mom," Olivia said. "Do you think my stomach looks fat?"

"I think you look great, honey," I said, though the truth was I hadn't really been able to drag my eyes away from those dots. If I ever had a reason to be on another billboard, I'd make I sure I was wearing a solid color, preferably black. I remembered the first time Jackson had seen a home video of himself ice skating. "That's not me. I skate better than that," he'd said. *That's not me,* I wanted to say. *I'm younger and prettier than that.*

"Isn't it great?" David said softly beside me.

Dickerman must have been watching us from his office window. I smelled stale tobacco smoke as he lumbered into the space between David and me. "Woo-ee," he said. "Did I say you could use my billboard?"

"Remember? It was your idea," David said. "Nice work, George."

"Dude," Justin said. "Bloody brilliant billboard, I must say."

"Totally," Caitlin said. "No wonder you're the boss."

David reached over and shook Dickerman's hand. "Well, George, great to see you. We'll be back in plenty of time for the show. So which one of you interns wants to do a drive-by with me to get the full effect?" The other interns and I fell into step with David. "Don't look back," he whispered.

"See Dick run," Olivia said.

"See us run faster," Caitlin said.

"Be nice," I said, though not with any real conviction. They didn't hear me anyway because they were already running.

"I call shotgun," Dickerman yelled from behind us just as David and I stepped onto the parking lot.

David pressed his keychain to unlock the doors of his battered Subaru, and the kids dove for the backseat. David and I stopped. "That's so not PC," I said when Dickerman wheezed his way up to us.

Dickerman wiped some long strands of hair from his face. "Okay, I call front seat." He leered at me. "But, hey, there's plenty of room on my lap, dollface."

There was truth in that unappealing statement. "Don't call me dollface," I said.

"Don't call her dollface," David said.

"Fine," Dickerman said. "I won't call her dollface. Now can I come?"

"You're the boss," David said. "But we'll have to take two cars."

But, of course, we didn't take two cars. Everyone wanted to ride together, so I drove. And I'm sure I'm not the only suburban woman who has cursed the day she bought her minivan, who has felt that ever since she bought it she's been in charge of transporting the world. Because she's always the one who has enough room to fit everybody for the soccer game or the camping trip or the shopping expedition. Maybe that was the real fantasy—someday I would own a sportscar, preferably foreign with a name that was all numbers and/or letters. S2000. Z3. TT. *Sorry, it's only a two-seater,* I'd say, and I'd wave to the kids and their friends or, in this case, Dickerman and the other chaperones. Then I'd open the passenger door and David would jump in. I'd press down on the accelerator and burn some unmotherly rubber as we rode off into the sunset together.

I allowed myself a small sigh. "Okay," I said, reaching around in the bottom of my bag for my keys. "Let's take the Caravan."

24

Anything you missed in college the first time

○ a. will still be there
○ b. is probably extinct by now
○ c. you found in other ways
○ d. will not be pretty if you try it in your
       forties

David easily managed to get to the passenger seat first, and the kids grabbed the three seats in the way back, so Dickerman had the middle seat all to himself. I turned around to face the back of the van. "Okay, everybody, buckle up."

"Dude, you sound just like my mother," Justin said.

"She sounds just like my mother, too," Olivia said. The three of them burst out laughing.

"Very funny," I said. "But I'm not going anywhere until everybody's buckled."

"She means it," Olivia said. "Trust me. I've known her for a long time."

"I've known you longer," I said.

"God, you're so competitive," Olivia said.

We circled out to the expressway and headed north. I was hoping the billboard and my fifteen minutes of fame might be a little bit easier to take whizzing by it at sixty-five miles per hour. Especially if I kept my eyes on the road. David was the first to see it. "Wow, will you look at that. Great visibility. This is going to make the show."

"Wow," Caitlin said from the back. "You can see those polka dots a mile away."

"Dude, that's a lot of spots," Justin said.

"Mom, can you go up to the next exit and turn around, so we can see it from the other side?"

●

"Okay, that's it," I said after the third double drive-by. "I'm going to run out of gas."

Dickerman leaned forward and put his hand on the back of my seat. "Oh, come on, Marge, just one more time."

"Yeah, Mrs. Marge, this totally rocks. And, dude, next time let's bring squirt guns. Five points a dot . . ."

"Don't you even think about it, Justin. Ever. Mom, come on, once more, okay?"

I looked over at David. He looked at his watch. "Jesus. Your show starts in three minutes."

The traffic heading south from Boston was just starting to back up. We'd never make it. "What are we going to do?" I asked, trying not to sound as panicked as I felt. How to blow your fifteen minutes of fame.

David stretched back in his seat and put his hands behind his head. "Don't worry. Somebody will just put on a CD or something until we get there. It used to happen all the time when there were two morning guys who hated each other."

"Wait a minute," Dickerman said. "Nobody ever told me that."

"That's because you're a maverick, George. Nobody wants to bother you with the small stuff." David turned back to me. "So the early guy would put a song on and leave three minutes early so their paths wouldn't cross. Then the next guy didn't think it was fair that the early guy's shift was shorter so he'd wait three minutes before he went in."

"Really?" I put on my blinker and moved over a lane. "They must have discovered all the long-playing songs."

"Yeah, lots of 'In-A-Gadda-Da-Vida.' And if they had to communicate, they'd leave notes like 'To the early morning person in the studio, please remember to leave the sports minutes in two distinct piles so that they are not inadvertently repeated in the course of a single morning.'"

Justin spoke up from the back. "'In-A-Gadda-Da-Vida,' dude, good song. Iron Butterfly, 1968, album version over seventeen minutes long. It was actually supposed to be 'In the Garden of Eden' but somebody got drunk and wrote the title down wrong, and then one of the record execs thought it sounded mystical, which was cool back then since the Beatles had everyone going to India, so they kept the title."

"Wow," David said.

"One of Justin's majors is entertainment trivia," I said.

"Maybe we can find a way to work it into your show," David said. "Then eventually we could give him his own spin-off trivia show. I mean, think about it, the sky's the limit."

Dickerman leaned forward and put a hand on each of our

seats. "I was thinking there might even be a show in there somewhere for me."

●

"Good afternoon," my daughter said with barely a tremble in her voice. "And welcome to *I'm Rubber, You're Glue*. My name is Olivia Monroe and I'm here with my, uh, my mother, March Monroe. And that's the only thing we're going to agree on for this whole show. So, if you're listening out there, call on in and bounce some questions off us, and we'll see how they stick."

Olivia had certainly borrowed all my best lines, but I didn't mind. She looked relaxed and confident, not at all rattled from the way we all had to run in from the parking lot. But it was more than that. I could almost believe she didn't mind doing the show with me.

Amazingly, three of the phone lights were flashing red. I pressed one. "Thanks for calling," I said. "You're on the air."

"Hi," the caller said. "I just wanted to tell you what a big fan I am of your show. It's really terrific and so are both of you."

Olivia and I looked at each other. I shrugged. "Thanks, Dad," Olivia said. "Have you seen us on the billboard yet? And, by the way, would you mind putting another hundred in my checking account? Either something is wrong with my ATM card or I'm out of money again."

I leaned closer to my microphone. "Don't you just hate the way college kids are only nice to you when they want money?"

"Oh, puh-lease," Olivia said into her microphone. "It's how we show our love. And, Dad, if you're still there, I want you to know you're going to be so happy for me. I found this really cheap airfare for spring break. It will hardly cost you anything."

Justin slid his chair a little closer to mine so he could reach my microphone. "Dude," he said. "Like where are you going for spring break?"

Caitlin stood up so she could reach Olivia's microphone. "I hear Daytona Beach sucks now but Panama City completely rocks."

It seemed like time to move along. I leaned over and pushed the other light on the phone. "Welcome to *I'm Rubber, You're Glue*," I said. "You're on the air."

"Greetings. This is Karyn, from *Karyn's Karmic Korner,* formerly live from this station in this very time slot. So, what, they wait till I leave to start using the billboard?"

"Karma is a boomerang," Olivia said.

"Bloody well said, Liv," Justin said.

I hated to be rude, but two more buttons were flashing. I pushed one. "Welcome to *I'm Rubber, You're Glue*. Hope you have something good to bounce off us today."

"I was just driving by and saw you on the billboard. That was the dress I really wanted for the wedding. Not the one you're wearing but the other one. Do you think we could have a couple more sessions? Just to go shopping and then maybe to get my stomach a little bit flatter?"

"I'm sorry but I can't seem to hear you," I said. "Guess we'll have to go to another caller." Olivia reached over and pushed the other button. "Hey," she said. "You're on the air."

"Hi, Olivia. Long time no hear."

Olivia looked at me, but I recognized the voice immediately. I leaned into the microphone. "Hi, Dana," I said.

"Oh hi, Dana," Olivia said. "Say hi to Layla for me, okay? Is there anything you want to bounce off us today?"

"Just want you and your mother to know that I saw the billboard. You're famous. Every single person from Rocky Point has to drive by it on the way in or out of Boston. But, I also called because I was wondering what you two think about people who keep their kitty litter in the oven."

I hung up on Dana, but I knew she'd get over it. We were pretty much friends for life.

David came into the conference room as soon as the show was over. "Great job," he said. "That phone was really hopping."

"Do you think anyone who didn't know us was listening?" I asked. "I mean, when will we get the numbers? We're going to need them in order to get some advertisers anyway, aren't we?"

"Numbers?" David asked. The kids had already started moving toward the door, but I was still sitting. He came over and leaned back against the table, facing me. "Numbers?" he said again. "Okay, next time you do the show, I'll run around and look in people's windows and count how many of them have their radios on."

I leaned back in my chair and fluffed my hair up a little. "Cute," I said.

"Jesus," Olivia said from the doorway. "Get a room."

●

Olivia's comment left us with one of those long silences that gets more awkward with every passing second. I was also assessing the warmth I was feeling, which seemed to be of the blush variety, though, once again, I wasn't completely sure. Finally, David put his hands on the table and pushed himself into a standing position. "You know," he said, "my wife drives a Dodge Caravan."

I started to laugh. "Your wife drives the same minivan as I do?"

"Pretty much. Hers is red, though."

"I had such a crush on you until you told me that." I looked at him. His eyes were still really blue, and I still liked his crooked smile. "Of course, my daughter telling us to get a room probably didn't help, either."

"Don't worry. I think she was just reacting to your getting more attention than she was."

"She's always had pretty good radar."

"Oh, that just gave me a great idea. Follow me."

He turned and pushed the door open and stood back so I could walk through first. I held my breath when I passed him, but felt a little surge of electricity anyway. We walked down the hallway side by side until we came to a door with a rectangular inset of glass. David opened it, and when we were both inside, he reached up for a string and pulled down some attic stairs. "After you," he said.

We ended up standing on the roof, staring into the mouth of a huge satellite dish. "What's that for?" I asked.

"AP comes through it. We feed them stories and take stories off it."

"Now?"

David laughed. "No. I brought you up here for the view. Isn't it great?"

I looked at him.

"Okay, well, anyway, I have to confess I had a crush on you, too, until I saw your minivan."

"Oh, God. Are we really going to talk about this?" I looked around for a comfortable place to sit. There wasn't even an uncomfortable place to sit, just a big, flat, pebble-studded tar roof.

"I think we just did." David walked over to the edge of the roof and sat down so his feet could hang over the edge.

I looked over the edge carefully to make sure I wasn't going to get dizzy. It was a one-story building. I probably could have jumped without getting hurt. I put my hand on David's shoulder and he reached up and held my arm until I was sitting safely beside him. "And so now what? On with the show?"

"Yeah, I think that's pretty much it. That and I guess I'll have to go back to Googling my high school girlfriends."

"Don't you mean ogling?"

"No. It means looking them up on Google.com and fantasizing about e-mailing them."

"You don't really e-mail them?"

"No, I don't think I even want to. I just like to think about it."

"Okay," I said. I dangled my feet and leaned forward just a little. Good thing it didn't look like there'd be enough drama that we'd have to consider jumping. If things had gone another way, we might have decided if we couldn't be together we didn't want to live at all. Then we would have stood up, held each other's hand, and hurled ourselves off the building, only to have stubbed a toe.

"March?" I'd almost forgotten David was still there, and his voice startled me. He put his hand on my forearm to steady me. "What are you thinking about?" he asked.

"I don't know," I said. "What are you thinking about?"

"I guess I was thinking, *Oh, well, we almost had Paris.*"

I looked straight ahead. "No, it was definitely Tuscany. I hear it's beautiful this time of year. Whatever time of year it is in Tuscany." I swung my legs back and forth a few times. "Do you think everyone our age is this pitiful? I mean, do you think, you know, that if you were married to me, you'd have a crush on your wife? Even if she does drive a minivan."

He laughed and I noticed his hand was still on my forearm. There was a nice heft to it. Maybe we could just come out and sit like this once in a while. "You might have something there. I heard somewhere that inertia is the biggest reason marriages fail. Actually, I got that from a Woody Allen movie."

The sun was starting to set over the highway, a big orange dot over Olivia's and my smaller dots on the billboard. "Which movie?" I asked.

"Damn, I forget the name. The one with the young girl who's in love with him, she's tall and thin . . ."

"That really narrows it down." I picked up a couple of pebbles and started throwing them off the roof. Maybe I'd luck out and Dickerman would walk by. "Well, we know what Woody did, but what do normal people do to save their marriages from inertia?"

David rubbed the fingertips of both hands back and forth along his jaw line, then picked up a few pebbles of his own. "I guess maybe you try to make things a little more exciting. You know, like we could surprise them by taking them out parking in the Caravans."

"Now there's a thought."

David smiled his crooked smile and leaned over and kissed me on the cheek.

"So, tell me," I asked, "how does that Google thing work again?"

25

> The best way to find what you really want is to follow your
>
> ○ a. instincts
> ○ b. heart
> ○ c. hormones
> ○ d. favorite designer

I hurried across my driveway and opened the side door. The mudroom was filled with red and white helium balloons. Pink ribbons trailed beneath them and were tied in a loose knot at the other end, holding them together in a bouquet. I pushed open the door to the kitchen. A banner draped from the paddle fan to the window over the kitchen sink proclaimed, CONGRATULATIONS DOTTY AND SPOTTY, YOU ROCK! All of the letters were made in the same thick black marker, but I could tell who'd made each of them. Jeff's were sure and steady, precisely formed. Jackson's were a little bit uneven, but the elaborate swirls of enthusiasm at the ends of each letter more than made up for it.

"Surprise!" Jeff and Jackson paraded in from the family room. They were smiling like twin game show hosts telling me I'd won the grand prize. I put an arm around each of them and pulled them in for a hug.

I managed to kiss Jackson on the cheek before he pulled away. "Me and Dad cooked dinner. We even have a vegetable." He ducked out into the mudroom and dragged the balloons past us and into the dining room. A couple of them conked us on our heads as they went by, and we all laughed.

I kissed Jeff on the lips and he kissed me back. "Thanks," I said. "I love you."

"You're welcome. I love you, too."

Jackson bounced back into the kitchen and opened the oven door. He looked inside for a minute, then closed it again. "We're good," he said.

"Smells delicious," I said. "You guys are the best. Is Olivia coming?"

Jeff shook his head. "She said she had homework." I looked at him. "Okay, actually she said, 'Earth to Dad. I don't live there anymore. Couldn't we celebrate at like Thanksgiving or something?'"

"That sounds more like it." I realized my feelings weren't even slightly hurt. Thanksgiving wasn't that far away and, after all, I saw more of my daughter than most mothers did at this stage. I hung up my car keys on one of the hooks on the back of the kitchen door. "Okay, you two, what can I do to help?"

"Not a thing, Mom. We live to serve. Go sit down and we'll bring it in to you."

"Wow, candles and everything," I yelled from my seat at the dining room table. "You guys sure know how to do it up right."

Jeff and Jackson patted each other on the back before they sat down at the table with me. I took a sip of my milk. I wouldn't have thought of serving potato puffs with steak and green beans. I knew the dollop of green ketchup on the center of each plate was Jackson's touch. I stabbed a puff with my fork and dipped it lightly. "See," Jackson said. "It tastes just like the red stuff."

As long as I closed my eyes, this was true. "Mmm," I said. "Just don't read me the ingredient list, okay?"

"So," Jeff said. "I almost went off the road on my way to work. Why didn't you tell me about the billboard?"

"I did. About eight times."

"Oh. That billboard."

Jackson snickered. "Good try, Dad."

Jeff took a long gulp of his milk, then took his time wiping his mustache with his napkin. "Sorry. I guess I was so focused on the school thing, I wasn't really hearing you about the radio station."

"It's just that it's so much more fun, and I think I could learn a lot. I was thinking I'd finish up the courses I started so I don't lose the credit. Who knows, I might want to take some production courses down the road. Maybe even public speaking or psychology or something." I pushed a green bean around on my plate. It was pretty soggy, but I managed to eat it anyway. "But in the meantime, I think the show has some real possibilities in terms of attracting advertisers and eventually getting syndicated."

Jeff was nodding his head as if he were really listening.

Jackson squirted a thick green line of ketchup down the center of his steak, then looked up. "You know, you should really consider bringing me on the show, too. Just in case Olivia starts to lose her edge."

"Okay," I said. "I'd love to have you. But you're the one who has to clear it with your sister."

"In a way," Jeff said, "it's like the way you haven't been listening to me about Flighty. I'd really like to breed her."

I forced myself to take a deep breath in, then out. I counted to ten in both English and Spanish. "You're kidding, right?" I finally said.

"No. I'm serious. It would be really interesting and I'd learn a lot. And maybe, eventually, I could make some money at it."

It seemed a lot like comparing apples to orangutans. But fair was fair and, besides, Jackson was watching. I knew one of the life lessons we should be teaching him was that relationships, the ones that last anyway, are really an extended game of *Let's Make a Deal*.

I allowed myself just one martyred sigh. "All right," I said. "But this isn't going to make me a grandmother or anything, is it?"

●

After Jackson cleared the table and disappeared into his room again, Jeff finished loading the dishwasher. I rummaged in the back of the refrigerator for the bottle of champagne I'd bought to celebrate the show with Jeff. Better late than never.

I shut the refrigerator door and held the bottle up for Jeff to see. He raised his eyebrows and we smiled at each other.

Jeff and I brought the champagne and our only two surviving champagne glasses up to our bedroom. When we were first married, a cousin of Jeff's, someone we'd never seen again after the wedding, had given us a set of eight. They were tall, narrow flutes, and even with hand-washing, it was remarkable that two had lasted this long. I put the glasses on my bedside table and Jeff put the bottle beside them.

Jeff ran his hands lightly along my back. "God," he said. "It's been a while."

The thing about having sex with the same person for twenty-two years of marriage, on top of another couple of particularly wonderful premarital years, was that you pretty much knew the territory. The upside was that you could tell just what this look or that touch or these words meant. This was also the downside. Like anything else you'd done many thousands of times, it didn't require your full concentration.

After all these years, I could still sometimes find myself completely turned on by my husband. We'd just look at each other and suddenly our eyes would catch. Or we'd be curled up on the couch together watching a movie, and the characters would do something that reminded us of us. Or, like tonight, we'd just know it was time. We'd been drifting and drifting away from each other, and this was the one reliable fix, not to mention a pretty good time.

But as the years turned into decades, I found myself occasionally slipping into automatic pilot. We'd be riding those waves of passion and, suddenly, I'd realize that a part of my brain had drifted off to compose a shopping list.

This wasn't one of those nights, at least not for me. I wondered afterward, as I almost always did, why we didn't do this more often. We rearranged the sheets and blankets, and leaned back against the headboard, sipping champagne and listening to the final songs of Eva Cassidy's *Live at Blues Alley* playing on the CD player on Jeff's side of the bed. Jeff raised an eyebrow and said, "Oh, yeah."

"God, you're so verbal," I said. I turned and kissed him, and he rubbed his mustache back and forth across my neck, something that had always kind of irritated me. I leaned away and took another sip of champagne.

"Okay, that was sublimely exquisite," he said. "Is that better?"

"Oh, yeah," I said.

Jeff took a sip of his champagne. Under the sheets he reached a leg over and hooked his ankle around mine.

I leaned my head on his shoulder. "Do you remember that rock festival we went to when we zipped our sleeping bags together and spent the night looking up at the stars? Wouldn't it be great if we could do that now?"

Jeff kissed the top of my head. "My back hurts just thinking about it."

"Come on, just try to be romantic for five more minutes."

Jeff rolled over and grabbed my hips with his thumbs resting just under my hipbones in the way I could never resist. "Okay," he said. "I'll try."

"Now where were we? . . . Okay, the sleeping bags are zipped together, and there are a million stars in the sky. And we're underneath, and you're wearing only a pair of boxers."

"You know I don't wear boxers."

"Just go with it." I kissed him on the sensitive spot on his neck, between his ear and his collarbone. "And I'm wearing a thong, black with lace maybe."

"Or polka dots?"

"Oh, God. All right, polka dots."

"Okay," my husband of twenty-two years said. "I'm with you."

multiple choice

CLAIRE COOK

A CONVERSATION WITH CLAIRE COOK

Q. You admit in your acknowledgment that you're "having a blast" as a novelist, but is it also a great deal of work? What are the pleasures and frustrations of your writing process? Can you describe a typical working day?

A. Having a blast as a novelist does not necessarily mean having a blast with the actual *writing*. The people part—meeting readers and booksellers and librarians and the media—is very social, and I'm having lots of fun with that. The writing part is great, too, once you get past the procrastination, the self-doubt, the feelings of utter despair. It's all of the stuff surrounding the writing that's hard. Once you find your zone, your place of flow, or whatever it is we're currently calling it, and lose yourself in the writing, it really is quite wonderful. I've heard writers say it's better than sex, though I'm not sure I'd go *that* far.

As for a typical working day, I've found that every day of my life presents me with dozens of perfectly valid reasons not to write. My kids, my house, my hair. And occasionally even more glamorous things like interviews and movie deals. So, for me, the only way to actually write a novel is to get really disciplined with myself. I write two pages a day, every day, or I'm not allowed to go to sleep. It gets ugly sometimes, but it works.

Q. Readers tend to assume that the narrator of a novel is a stand-in for the author. Do you relate to anyone in particular in Multiple Choice? *When writing, how much do you draw from your own life?*

A. I relate to all of the characters, both two- and four-legged, in my novels. I think you have to, at least to some degree, in order to write the characters. It's all about being a good eavesdropper, and it's all grist for the mill. I've always been that person at the restaurant listening to the conversation at the next table. It's nice to finally have found a career where that becomes nondeviant behavior. I'm also pleased to have a job where making things up is encouraged, since I've always had a tendency to rewrite events to make them more interesting even as they're happening.

Q. Do you feel that your characters' journeys are complete at the novel's end, or do they live on? Would you return to previous characters in future work?

A. I love books that don't wrap everything up too neatly at the end, and I think it's a big compliment to hear that a reader is left wanting more. After each novel, I hear from many readers asking for a sequel—they say they just *have* to find out what will happen to these people next. I think it's wonderful that the characters have come to life for them. But, for now, I think I'll grow more as a writer by trying to create another group of quirky characters. Maybe a few books down the road, I'll feel ready to return to some of them—who knows?

Q. Jeff and March spend a good deal of their time miscommunicating and missing each other. However, you end the novel with a very intimate scene between the two of them. Can you discuss your reasons for doing so? As an author and wife, how difficult is it to maintain a realistic yet affecting sense of romance, both in life and on the page?

A. Hmm . . . it's quite possible that I might have imagined the part about couples spending that much time miscommunicating. Certainly, my husband and I never do.

I think the dance of a long-term relationship is pretty complicated. Again, not from any personal experience, but I hear it's quite possible to love someone very much one minute and be driven completely crazy by that same person the next. We ask a lot from our married partners—romance/security, lover/best friend. You sweep the floors with the same person who's supposed to sweep you off your feet. I've often thought it would make more sense for couples to live next door to each other, just to keep some of the mystery alive.

Q. "It just wasn't the life I'd expected. I supposed every woman my age had moments of longing for the things she imagined she missed," March confesses. Are there any opportunities in your own life that you feel you sacrificed in order to be a good parent or wife? If so, do you intend to return to any of those plans as your characters did?

A. I already have returned to those plans. Being a novelist is the thing I almost missed. Although, in hindsight, I think I used my kids as an excuse for not writing that first book until I was in my forties. But all's well that ends well, and I'm thrilled I finally got up the nerve to do it. So many women have written to say that my story has been an inspiration to them, and I hope that's true.

Q. Etta says to March, "We simply didn't have as many choices. Your world is more complicated, I'm afraid." Is this multiplicity of choice both the benefit and drawback of the feminist move-

ment? What do you think that means for women of Olivia's generation?

A. Well, some of it is that our world is just so much more complicated for everybody. I think we're all a little bit overwhelmed right now by all the choices. Just trying to figure out what cell phone plan to pick is a full-time job.

Yes, it is true that Etta didn't have as many choices back then, but look at all the choices she has now. I spoke to an eighty-year-old woman recently who'd finally sold her big family home and moved into a smaller place, and she was trying to decide how she could best challenge herself during the next phase of her life. She was *eighty*! Isn't that great?

She'd led a very traditional Mom-stays-at-home kind of life until her kids were grown-up, but in the last thirty or so years, she'd earned a couple of degrees, written a book, traveled all over the world. In my teens, I thought women just stopped existing after their kids moved out. I now can see how much fun there is down the road.

I worry sometimes that the women of Olivia's generation will go down in history as the entitled generation. Their grandmothers couldn't have it all, their mothers struggled to try to have it all, and now they're just absolutely convinced that they deserve it all. Great self-esteem though—I'll give them that.

Q. The heroines of your novels share some common traits—for example, a vague dissatisfaction with their lives but also the nerve to do something about it. What is it about the female experience that produces the bravery and humor displayed in your characters? Do you think women are more prone than men to sacrifice for their relationships and family?

A. I'm fascinated by people in transition, and if you're not dissatisfied with some aspect of your life, vaguely or otherwise, you wouldn't bother to change anything. It's just too much work.

I think the male experience is pretty funny, too. I just feel better equipped to write about things from a woman's point of view.

Certainly, there are exceptions, and men and women give in different ways, and I like men a lot, really I do but, yes, I think women are more prone than men to put their own lives on the back burner while they nurture others. Partly, it's because they're so good at multitasking. Either that or it's because men are so good at pretending they're not good at multitasking.

Q. *Warmth and comedy are the highlights of* Multiple Choice, *as is true of all your novels. Are there any writers you admire for their wit or insight? If so, how has their writing influenced you?*

A.Whenever I'm doing a book event, someone in the audience inevitably asks, "Who are your favorite writers?" and I always say, "The ones who've been nice to me."

I admire many, many writers for their wit and insight, but I think it's only fair to single out two who've been particularly generous as mentors and friends: Mameve Medwed and Jeanne Ray. Fortunately, they both happen to be very talented—and funny—so if you've somehow missed their books, you should read them immediately.

Q. *You keep an active Web diary available to your readers, and you encourage them to contact you. Does the Web site help you better understand your audience? How do reader reactions affect your work?*

A. My favorite comment from a reader, and one that I hear all the time, is, "Ohmigod, you're writing my life!" It's great to be reassured that I'm on the right track. I also love that the comment comes from such a wide variety of people—it cuts across lines of age, occupation, ethnicity, geographical location, and even gender. I like to think that I'm writing a slice of all of our lives, and I feel very connected to my readers, and often feel that I'm writing this for all of us. And I never forget for a minute that, without readers, I wouldn't have a job!

I've received, and answered, thousands of e-mails from readers, and what I love about my Web site, www.clairecook.com, is that it makes it so easy for readers to communicate with me. I'm also incredibly grateful to these same readers who have forwarded my newsletter, attended my book events, and talked me up to their families and friends. There are a lot of books out there, and readers are a huge part of the reason that mine have done so well.

Q. When did you first know you were a writer?

A. When I was three. My mother entered me in a contest to name the Fizzies whale, and I won in my age group. It's quite possible that mine was the only entry in my age group since "Cutie Fizz" was enough to win my family a six-month supply of Fizzies tablets (root beer was the best flavor) and a half dozen turquoise plastic mugs with removable handles. At six I had my first story on the Little People's Page in the Sunday paper (about Hot Dog, the family Dachshund) and at sixteen I had my first front page feature in the local weekly.

I majored in film and creative writing in college, and fully expected that the day after graduation a brilliant novel would emerge, fully formed, like giving birth. When that didn't happen, I felt like an impostor. Looking back, I can see that I had to live my life so I'd have something to write about. Decades later, I have no shortage of material.

Q. What ideas do you explore in your novels?

A. I don't really think about my writing that way. For me, it all starts with the characters, so I'm always surprised when I'm introduced at a book event, and I hear, "Claire Cook writes about relationships." Or transitions or suburbia or family. I thought I was writing about the Hurlihys or the Monroes! But I suppose I am fascinated by people and by relationships, and I'm particularly drawn to characters in transition. That's where you find the fireworks—people trying to let go of something and move on to something else are often messy and always interesting.

Q. Must Love Dogs *is now a Warner Bros. feature film starring Diane Lane, John Cusack, Christopher Plummer, Elizabeth Perkins, Dermot Mulroney, and Stockard Channing. What was that experience like for you? How did it happen? Since the movie always involves changes to the book, was that difficult for you to handle?*

A. First of all, yes, it's a movie! Woo-hoo! Many books are optioned for film, and how lucky am I to have mine turn out to be one of the very few that actually make it to the big screen? And what a truly amazing cast! By the way, not only are they talented, but they were all extraordinarily kind to my family and me. They even autographed my director's chair to surprise me! (For on-set photos, see my blog at www.clairecook.com.)

The way it happened was that Gary David Goldberg, who created *Spin City, Family Ties*, and *Brooklyn Bridge*, read the book and decided he wanted to make the movie. He's really talented and funny, and also an extremely nice guy, and I knew early on that with Gary writing, directing, and producing, my novel was in the best of hands.

It was an amazing and joyful experience for me. I had a

great time watching everyone's vision of my book develop. It's such a collaborative medium, and it was fascinating to see how each person adds a layer, from the writer to the director to the actors to the cinematographer to the set designer to the producers. Also, the way I see it is that *Must Love Dogs* will remain on the bookshelves intact, and the movie will help lots of new readers discover the novel.

Q. Has Multiple Choice *been optioned for a movie yet?*

A. Yes! Working Title (*Fargo, Love Actually, Bridget Jones's Diary*) has optioned *Multiple Choice* for a feature film They've made so many fabulous, quirky movies, and I can't wait to see what they do with my third novel!

QUESTIONS
FOR DISCUSSION

1. March Monroe is returning to college to complete her degree many years after leaving school to marry Jeff and raise a family. What are her feelings toward the decisions she made as a young woman? What are her feelings about returning to school as an adult?

2. There are few events in life that we get a chance to do over again. If you could relive any aspect of your youth—knowing what you know now—would you do it? What would you do differently and why?

3. March says that "relationships, the ones that last anyway, are really an extended game of *Let's Make A Deal*." How do the various relationships in *Multiple Choice* prove that quote either true or false? Do you find it true in your own experience? Can you think of any other game title that March might have used?

4. Are there any Ahndrayuhs in your neighborhood? How about David Callahans in your workplace? And—tell the truth—are there thongs in your underwear drawer? Is your husband a boxer or a briefs man?

5. After March's radio show, she stops to buy dinner on the way home and hopes the woman ringing up her purchases will recognize her voice. Have you ever had a moment of almost fame like that, when you thought the world might stand up and take notice, but it didn't quite turn out that way? Do you still dream of fifteen minutes of fame? Would you settle for five?

6. The phrase "karma is a boomerang" appears several times in the course of the book. Do you believe this is true? Does March? Give some examples of March's karma-related behavior.

7. When book groups meet to discuss *Must Love Dogs*, they often serve Sarah's winey macaroni and cheese, made without butter and with white wine instead of milk, and served in wine glasses for best effect. What might your book group, real or imagined, serve when discussing *Multiple Choice*?

8. "I'd spent so many years doing things I didn't really want to do for people I didn't really like." Do you think this speaks to March's need to please people or is it about time management? Or is it both? Is this quote true for most women? Do you think we all reach a point in our lives when we realize we don't want to be all things to all people?

9. Mothers and daughters share a complicated and profound union, built on years of mutual observation. How do March and Olivia demonstrate their intimate knowledge of each other's behaviors and needs during the course of the book? In what ways are they strangers?

10. What do you think Claire Cook should write about in her next novel?

Don't miss this excerpt from Claire Cook's novel

MUST LOVE DOGS

Available in paperback and now

a major motion picture starring

Diane Lane, Christopher Plummer,

and John Cusack

I decided to listen to my family and get back out there. "There's life after divorce, Sarah," my father proclaimed, not that he'd ever been divorced.

"The longer you wait, the harder it'll be" was my sister Carol's little gem, as if she had some way of knowing whether or not that was true.

After months of ignoring them, responding to a personal ad in the newspaper seemed the most detached way to give in. I wouldn't have to sit in a restaurant with a friend of a friend of one of my brothers, probably Michael's, but maybe Johnny's or Billy Jr.'s, pretending to enjoy a meal I was too nervous to taste. I needn't endure even a phone conversation with someone my sister Christine had talked into calling me. My prospect and I would quietly connect on paper or we wouldn't.

HONEST, HOPELESSLY ROMANTIC, old-fashioned gentleman seeks lady friend who enjoys elegant dining, dancing and the slow bloom of affection. WM, n/s, young 50s, widower, loves dogs, children and long meandering bicycle rides.

The ad jumped out at me the first time I looked. There wasn't much competition. Rather than risk a geographic jump to one of the Boston newspapers, I'd decided it was safer and less of an effort to confine my search to the single page of classifieds in the local weekly. Seven towns halfway between Boston and Cape Cod were clumped together in one edition. Four columns of "Women Seeking Men." A quarter of a column of "Men Seeking Women," two entries of "Women Seeking Women," and what was left of that column was "Men Seeking Men."

I certainly had no intention of adding to the disheartening surplus of heterosexual women placing ads, so I turned my attention to the second category. It was composed of more than its share of control freaks, like this guy—*Seeking attractive woman between 5'4" and 5'6", 120–135 lbs., soft-spoken, no bad habits, financially secure, for possible relationship*. I could picture this dreamboat making his potential relationships step on the scale and show their bank statements before he penciled them in for a look-see.

And then *this* one. Quaint, charming, almost familiar somehow. When I got to *the slow bloom of affection*, it just did me in. Made me remember how lonely I was.

I circled the ad in red pen, then tore it out of the paper in a jagged rectangle. I carried it over to my computer and typed a response quickly, before I could change my mind:

Dear Sir:
  You sound too good to be true, but perhaps we could have a cup of coffee together anyway—at a public place. I am a WF, divorced, young 40, who loves dogs and children, but doesn't happen to have either.
                                            —*Cautiously Optimistic*

I mailed my letter to a Box 308P at the *County Connections* offices, which would, in turn, forward it. I enclosed a small check to secure my own box number for responses. Less than a week later I had my answer:

Dear Madam,

Might I have the privilege of buying you coffee at Morning Glories in Marshbury at 10 AM this coming Saturday? I'll be carrying a single yellow rose.

—*Awaiting Your Response*

The invitation was typed on thick ivory paper with an actual typewriter, the letters *O* and *E* forming solid dots of black ink, just like the old manual of my childhood. I wrote back simply, *Time and place convenient. Looking forward to it.*

I didn't mention my almost-date to anyone, barely even allowed myself to think about its possibilities. There was simply no sense in getting my hopes up, no need to position myself for a fall.

I woke up a few times Friday night, but it wasn't too bad. It's not as if I stayed up all night tossing and turning. And I tried on just a couple of different outfits on Saturday morning, finally settling on a yellow sweater and a long skirt with an old-fashioned floral print. I fluffed my hair, threw on some mascara and brushed my teeth a second time before heading out the door.

Morning Glories is just short of trendy, a delightfully overgrown hodgepodge of sun-streaked greenery, white lattice and round button tables with mismatched iron chairs. The coffee is strong and the baked goods homemade and delicious. You could sit at a table for hours without getting dirty looks from the people who work there.

The long Saturday-morning take-out line backed up to the door, and it took me a minute to maneuver my way over to the tables. I scanned quickly, my senses on overload, trying to pick out the rose draped across the table, to remember the opening line I had rehearsed on the drive over.

"Sarah, my darlin' girl. What a lovely surprise. Come here and give your dear old daddy a hug."

"Dad? What are *you* doing here?"

"Well, that's a fine how-do-you-do. And from one of my very favorite daughters at that."

"Where'd you get the rose, Dad?"

"Picked it this morning from your dear mother's rose garden. God rest her soul."

"Uh, who's it for?"

"A lady friend, honey. It's the natural course of this life that your dad would have lady friends now, Sarry. I feel your sainted mother whispering her approval to me every day."

"So, um, you're planning to meet this lady friend here, Dad?"

"That I am, God willing."

Somewhere in the dusty corners of my brain, synapses were connecting. "Oh my God. Dad. *I'm* your date. I answered your personal ad. I answered my own father's personal ad." I mean, of all the personal ads in all the world I had to pick this one?

My father looked at me blankly, then lifted his shaggy white eyebrows in surprise. His eyes moved skyward as he cocked his head to one side. He turned his palms up in resignation.

"Well, now, there's one for the supermarket papers. Honey, it's okay, no need to turn white like you've seen a ghost. Here. This only proves I brought you up to know the diamond from the riffraff."

Faking a quick recovery is a Hurlihy family tradition, so I squelched the image of a single yellow rose in a hand other than my father's. I took a slow breath, assessing the damage to my heart. "Not only that, Dad, but maybe you and I can do a Jerry Springer show together. How 'bout 'Fathers Who Date Daughters'? I mean, this is big, Dad. The Oedipal implications alone—"

"Oedipal, smedipal. Don't be getting all college on me now, Sarry girl." My father peered out from under his eyebrows. "And lovely as you are, you're even lovelier when you're a smidgen less flip."

I swallowed back the tears that seemed to be my only choice besides flip, and sat down in the chair across from my father. Our waitress came by and I managed to order a coffee. "Wait a minute. You're not a young fifty, Dad. You're sixty-six. And when was the last time you rode a bike? You don't own a bike. And you hate dogs."

"Honey, don't be so literal. Think of it as poetry, as who I am in the bottom of my soul. And, Sarah, I'm glad you've started dating again. Kevin was not on his best day good enough for you, sweetie."

"I answered my own father's personal ad. That's not dating. That's sick."

My father watched as a pretty waitress leaned across the table next to ours. His eyes stayed on her as he patted my hand and said, "You'll do better next time, honey. Just keep up the hard work." I watched as my father raked a clump of thick white hair away from his watery brown eyes. The guy could find a lesson in . . . Jesus, a date with his *daughter*.

"Oh, Dad, I forgot all about you. You got the wrong date, too. You must be lonely without Mom, huh?"

The waitress stood up, caught my father's eye and smiled. She walked away, and he turned his gaze back to me. "I think about her every day, all day. And will for the rest of my natural life. But don't worry about me. I have a four o'clock."

"What do you mean, a four o'clock? Four o'clock Mass?"

"No, darlin'. A wee glass of wine at four o'clock with another lovely lady. Who couldn't possibly hold a candle to you, my sweet."

I supposed that having a date with a close blood relative was far less traumatic if it was only one of the day's two dates. I debated whether to file that tidbit away for future reference, or to plunge into deep and immediate denial that the incident had ever happened. I lifted my coffee mug to my lips. My father smiled encouragingly.

Perhaps the lack of control was in my wrist. Maybe I merely forgot to swallow. But as my father reached across the table with a pile of paper napkins to mop the burning coffee from my chin, I thought it even more likely that I had simply never learned to be a grown-up.